The Hunt

Cecile Paya

Copyright © 2024 by Cecile Paya

All rights reserved.

No portion of this book may be reproduced in any form without written permission from the publisher or author, except as permitted by U.S. copyright law.

Contents

one

February 2020

"Detective Baptise"

Nyla looked up at her partner Matt who had a serious look on his face.

Matt was about 6'2 he was a big guy look like he can be someone body-guard. He has light green eyes and warm tan skin.

"We have another case near downtown" he spoke with a lazy tone.

"Okay" I replied getting up and fixing the case files on my desk tying to make sure everything was neat.

"Is everything alright Matt" I asked trying to catch up with his fast pace.

" Yeah just ready to go home to my wife and kids" he replied with a sigh

"Can you slow down..damn" I laughed .

"I sometimes forget how short you are" he. playful pushed me causing me to almost fall .

Matt was like a big brother to me. I have no siblings so I'm excited that a have someone to call my brother.

"Now you know you too damn big to be pushing me"

—

"Can we get this tapped off" I politely asked the female officer because once the body was discovered this should have already been done .

As I walk over to the other detectives I see a women in the dumpster with a blanket covering her body .

Smells like she been here for some time.

"Do we have any identification" I asked Detective Day trying to get a better look at the women. She was bound and gagged.

"No not yet...whoever did this cut off her finger tips and pulled her teeth out" she respond with a hurt look in her eyes.

"Did anyone come forward about who they think this is" I responded with a sigh.

If we can't identify who this person is we don't have nothing about this case.

"Yes..It's a family over there who think this could be they mother" she pointed behind the yellow tape at a family who was holding on to each other crying.

I walked over there already prepare myself that i might have to tell them that this is they loved one .

—

Matt pulled the body out of the dumpster to find out that she was beaten and she was stripped naked .

He was trying to find anything that can identify this women.

Matt called the Forensic pathologists to examine the body.

As she rolled her over on her back they see a tattoo on her back that says "Crybaby"

Now Matt has something.

As I was trying to calm down the family I hear someone walking towards my way.

"I found a tattoo on her bck that says "Crybaby" he tells me in my ear .

I nod my head as my way of saying thank you.

Matt walks back over towards the scene trying to find more evidence.

"Does your mother has any distinctive marks on her body" I asked what looks like the older daughter who is holding a sleeping baby.

"I-umm i dont t-think so" he replied trying to talk through her tears as they continue to fall .

"My momma has a tattoo" the younger son responded as he clears his throat as he tried to hold his tears.

"Do you know where sweetie" I spoke in soft voice.

"Y-yeah umm on her back" he looks down at the ground as he talk.

Something told me this was going to be there mother and I was going to have to tell them that's her.

"What does it say"

"Crybaby" he whispered

two

I cleared my throat "Can you repeat that for me" I asked again to make sure I heard that right

"Crybaby" he repeated looking at me with watery eyes.

"I'm sorry to tell you this but it's y-" in the middle of my sentence the daughter just broke down crying.

"NOOOO" she screamed

I went under the tape to help stable her and make sure her baby is okay as she continue to yell.

"Who did this to her" the younger son asked as he hugged his sister.

"That's what we trying to find out"

"I know he d-did it..he killed m-my fucking momma" she stuttered

"Matt" I called out for him.

"Yeah" he responded looking at the crying family.

"Can you take them down to headquarters and make sure they okay"

"Yeah.. come on guys" he told them

"And Matt..Can you find out who exactly he is" he nodded saying yes

— My phone started ringing and I see the caller Id was Matt.

"Hello" I answered

"The mother name is Monica Western she's 53 years old"

Monica had been in the streets for 5 years now. She just started doing drugs with her bff that goes by the name G-Baby.

As Matt continue to tell me about Monica he tells me that Monica and G-Baby would always get into fights. G-Baby would sometimes force Monica into drugs. He would always tell her if she leaves him he would kill her himself.

With me receiving that information G-Baby is my number one suspect right now.

"Do you know G-Baby real name" I asked Matt ask I walk away from the now cleared scene.

"No she said that he would always go as G-Baby not his real name" Matt told me as I run my hand down my face.

"Okay Thanks"

"No Problem" he responded —I walk around the neighborhood trying to find anyone who can tell me what happened to Monica.

Nobody was talking and it was getting annoying because I know someone knows something and they wasn't talking. It was like they was scared.

I head to my car irritated asf right about now.

As I get in my car I get a family group called. I smiled answering my phone. I really did miss my parents.

"Hola papá" I spoke to my father

"Hola madre" I spoke to my mother

My mother is African American and my father is Columbian which makes me Afro -Colombian. As a child my parents would always teach me about both of their heritage. Some kids would hate to learn but me I was soo involved with my parents childhood and where they came from it was just so interesting to me .

"Hola pequeño" I smiled rolling my eyes as my dad called me my childhood name.

"Dad i'm not little anymore" I groaned

"Your my still my little girl" He smiled in the camera with his pearly white teeth.

Michael, my dad, has black curly hair with a little bit of grey mixed. He has dark blue eyes with his smooth caramel skin .You wouldn't think he was 48 if you looked at him.

"Okay papá" I played rolled my eyes and smiled.

"Mama" I called into the phone.

"Lala baby what" She smiled as she laid her had on my dad shoulder with her beautiful smile.

Katherine, my mamma, has big beautiful hair that I always adored. She has doe-brown eyes and a queenly figure. My momma is literally my bff,She is 46.

As we continued our conversation,eventually I had to hang up. We said I love yous as I was pulling up at headquarters.—"What does the autopsy say" I asked Matt

"She was strangled and beaten, It seems like she was tortured and she was stuffed with artificial drugs" he spoke as he looked down at the autopsy.

"She was in that dumpster for a about 8-10 days..that explains the smell"

"That's sickening" I expressed with a disgusting face

"Yeah we have to find this G-Baby guy" Matt responded

"Do you have any leads" Matt asked

"No" I shook my head with a sigh

" I will find some leads" He spoke as if he was sure

"What makes you think that" I asked with a raised eyebrow

He looked over at me with that same blank face.

"I have my ways"

three

----

4 weeks later

March 2020

Its 3 in the morning and I'm still at the headquarters trying to find James aka G-Baby.

Everyday after my shift I will late and try to find James. She deserves justice who can do this to someone.

As I was looking over the information that Matt somehow got I heard something.I look up soo fucking fast because I know I'm in here alone.

I started to get up but I see Matt.

"Matt what the hell" I breathe out .

"Ohh I didn't think anyone was here" He replied looking truly surprised.

"Yeahh I'm still trying to find James" I replied putting down the file looking over at him.

"Why you still here" I asked him really wondering why he still here.

"I left something in my office" He replied

"At 3 in the m-you know what that's not my business" I replied fixing up everything before I leave to head home.

As I head out the door I told Matt goodnight.—

I wonder why your love is so toxicFour deep in the rental to give you this ten, came from a rock-headI watched Lil Joe roll up an opp soon as he got backThey was talking until we pulled up, turned they block to library They beggin' for me to drop a tape, I'm sorry to my fansFuck halftime,my youngins pulled up fa two bands Leaking my song, back to the booth, I gotta go ten times harder

I rapped to No Fentanyl/ Camera Roll by Rylo Rodriguez as I drive home.

I turned the car off grabbing the key that goes to my house so i dont have to stand outside trying to find the correct key.

Before I got out I looked around to make sure I'm safe, ain't tryna get snatch up.

I unlocked my door and called out to my dog Dino. His nickname is Nugget.

I hear little nails against the hard floor.

"Hey stink" I coo at my luh DinoNugget

He just jumped around with his little tongue hang out looking cute as ever.

"Let's go eat and afterwords Im going to take youu to potty...okay" I talked to him as if he understood.

I fixed his food on one side and water on the other side.

"Eat" I commanded rubbing behind his ear

I walked into the kitchen washing my hands.It's 4 almost 5 in the morning so I won't eat anything heaving. —

i see yah reading but not voting . what's up with that? do ii gotta hit someone in da throat assum . lmk

dont forget to vote and comment okay . i really wanna know what yah think abtt this . should i continue or not ?

four

I woke up to someone pushing me faintly hearing them telling me to wakeup .

"What df you want mane" I replied drained.

"Goodmorning Mari" My homeboy Tay responded smartly.

"It's 7:23..We gon be late for school" He told me as he walk towards my window opening my curtains.

"□□□ □□□ □□□ □□□..□□□□□□" I signed with my hands as I rubbed my ear that was slightly buzzing.

"□□□□ □□□□ □□□□□ □□" He signed bck as he walked out my room.

I moved the covers off my body sitting up just looking at my wall.

I just sat here for a good 5 minutes really thinking about my life rn. Like Why do I have SSHL ? Why me out of all people, Why my parents never wants me around ? Is it because my SSHL ?

SSHL -Sudden sensorineural (inner ear) hearing loss or commonly known as sudden deafness is an unexplained rapid loss of hearing either all at once or over a few days.

Sudden deafness frequently affects only one ear.

I get up and do my routine trying to make sure ion look too bad.

Me and Tay has been friends since 3rd grade.He's a brother to me more than anything.He was always there for me making sure I was straight.

"MAR MAR" Tay yelled trying not to be too loud.

"Coming" I replied softly.

As I walked down the stairs I see Tay eating and a plate of food that he must have made.

Tay parents sadly died when he was 9 years old. He never talks about how they died,every time I asked he just change the subject or tells me to drop it.

"□□□□□□" I signed.

He just smiled and nodded his head.

—"I honestly hate school" I say to myself as we pulled up

Garvey HighSchool

Garvey HighSchool is like your typical highschool. You have nerds and the "popular"people.

As I get out the car and walk inside the school building I faintly heard the school bell ring.

Literally nobody was moving like they have to be in class. The halls was still full of students talking and laughing.

"Have a good day Mari" Tay told me as we hugged going our separate ways.

I really just want to turn back around and walk out this door. I'm already tired of school.

"Goodmorning" The school security guard spoked at he pat me down. As others make they way through the metal detector.

"Goodmorning" I responded

I made my way through the metal detector and the pat down without a problem. I dont even carry books let alone a damn pencil. I just come to school with nothing but myself.

Everyday you would get pat down AND walk through the metal detector before heading into class.

They obviously wasn't doing they job right or some because someone is always smoking in the damn bathroom.

Im slowly walking to class because I mean shit, im already late and ion even want to be here but I started speeding up once I realized all eyes gon be on me as soon as I opened the door if im last going in.

"Let this day go smoothly" I silently prayed before opening the door.

five

I knew Mondays was terrible but not this damn terrible.

1st period teacher Ms.Ray dont know when to hush. It's too early in the morning for her to be talking this much .

2nd period wasn't bad, we had a sub and you know they dont be doing they job.

3rd period was advanced science courses my favorite class.

4th period is lunch.—"Dooda" Tay walked up and hugged me

"Dont call me that here" I mugged him

"My fault"

"How was class" He asked getting his food tray

"Boring as always" I lightly shrugged my shoulders

"I have something to handle so I wont be going home with you"

"What time would you be back" I replied as I picked with my food

"I dont know honestly" he mumbled

"Alright just be safe Tayvon" I worriedly told him

"I will" He replied kissing my forehead — The rest of school went okay even though I almost wanted to punch everyone who started looking at me.

As the last bell ring I get up pulling my pants even though they gon fall back down.

"Aye nigga watch were you going" Some nigga replied

"My fault" I mumbled trying to get out the way

"Yo deaf ass" He replied pulling my hearing aid out

"Can you stop playing dude I said my fault" I spoke as I could barely hear myself out of my left ear.

"Bump into me again...fuck you up" He replied as I tried to read his lips.

"Okay" I mumbled rubbing my ear

"Can you give it back now" I held out my hand

"Here" he tossed it crossed the room making the people he hang around with laugh like some shit was funny.

"Now if I come back tmr with a gun and blow this bitch up I'll be wrong" I responded lowly as I walked over towards the windows and pick it up

"Bitch" He pushed me causing me to drop my hearing aid stepping on it in the process.

"Fuck" I semi yelled looking at my now broken hearing aid that Tay work soo hard to pay for.

I picked up my hearing aid speeding out the class as I hear them laughing at me. I felt a tear run down my face as I'm walking out the build.

"Fuck ass school" I mumbled walking home.

SIX

We finally found him.

He was hiding out in some abandoned apartments.He was hold-ing a picture in his hand of a little girl who could have been 12 years old.

"He's in the room 5"

"Thanks Detective Day" I replied walking to towards the interrogation room 5 with a pen and a notebook.

"You dont want your partner with you" She asked

"No I think he's working on another cases rn"—"I'm Detective Baptise" I introduced myself as I sit down infront of him.

He just looks up at me holding the same picture.

"You know your guilty for the murder of Monica Western right" I told him folding my hands in-front of me as I leaned forward.

Again.Nothing

"Why did you do it" I asked

"I didn't" He replied

"We have witnesses James...You also have motive "I told him with a raised eyebrow

"I-I just hit her" He replied looking down

"You did more than just hit her" I responded

"I swear that's all I did" He responded as he started crying

"Clean yourself up" I responded giving him some tissue.

"Just knock on the door once your ready" I responded walking out.—It's been almost a hour, I know I said when you ready but damn sir.

I pulled my phone out my pocket and started scrolling on instagram because why not.

□□□□□□□_□

Liked by □□□□□□□□□□ and 5,476 others□□□□□□□_□: This is the way I live□View all 130 comments □□□□□□□□□□:my heart

Me and Cylo was dating for about 7 months but realized we better off as friends so our relationship ended on a good note. I see he has a beautiful girlfriend now and living life. I love that for him.

As I continue to scroll on my instagram timeline I see Matt walking towards me from the corner of my eye.

"How is it going" He asked with his hands in his pocket pointing his head towards room 5.

"Everything is good" I responded putting my phone back in my pocket.

"Has he confessed yet"

"No he started crying so I let him have his time"I shrugged

"....and how long was that" He asked with a raised eyebrow.

"A hour ago" I checked watch.

"Do you think he's going to tell you anything"

"Yes he started crying which means he's feeling guilty" I got up from my desk.

"I'm going in to see if he's willing to talk now"

"Goodluck" Matt responded with a low chuckle

don't forget to vote and comment.

lmk what you think.

seven

"Are you okay now"I asked walking into the room.

He just looked at me with red eyes.

"Are you ready to talk about what happened again" I spoke sitting down.

He nodded yes

"I'm ready when you are" I responded as I pulled out my notebook and pen for the second time.

"Me and Monica was happy okay...I-I may have force her into drugs and other terrible things" He whispered.

"I might have did and said bad things but i loved her" He started crying again.

"Aht no stop crying and keep talking" I told him as I kept writing down everything he said.

"Keep going"

"I had joined this gang thing I really dont know what it is...but I just needed money for my little girl"He showed me the picture of who I assume is his daughter.

"The money was good,I been working there for almost 6 years now"

"I just wanted to be happy with Monica and my little girl again that's all" He replied wiping his eyes.

"It went to just watching them make drugs,to transporting it,than selling it."

"Monica wasn't meant to be in this situation but we started using the products...getting high"

"I dont know who the guy is put I told him I wanted to leave to be with my family more"He replied shaking his head.

"In order for me to leave I had to kill the one I love the most...b-but I couldn't kill her.So he took my daughter as his way of threatening me."

"So I started beating on Monica trying to kill her but I just couldn't do that.When I called him off the burner phone and told him that I couldn't he just simply said "This is your fault".

"Where is the phone now" I asked

"He took it once he was done" he whispered

"He arrived at the location,He tortured her in-front of me like I wasn't there at all" He put his hands on face as he cried.

"I-I should have helped her b-but I was worried about my little girl..he was going to kill her,I just know he would."

"Do you have any description of this guy" I asked once he calmed down.

"No...sorry"

"Once everything was done did you ever get your daughter back" I asked

"No...since I couldn't kill Monica he killed her,that was my punishment"

"I'm sorry" I responded truly sorry about what happened to his daughter.

"Do you know where this place is located"I asked

"It's by the g-"

He couldn't finish his sentence because Matt walked into the room.

"Come out here let's talk" He told me as he held the door open for me.

I get up and walk out the room with an attitude.

"What do you possibly want" I asked clearly annoyed.

"I was just trying to see if he told you anything that's all" He responded with his hands in his pocket.

"He could have if yo big ass didnt walk through the door"I rolled my eyes.

"I was going to tell you that you can go home now it's 9"

"After this yeah I would go home" I told him.

"NO..Im sorry I mean no, you been here all day I know your tired"

"I mean yeah but I got this"

"Yeah I know you do okay just let me take over"

"Okay fine...Make sure he give you that location we can go check it out tmr" I told him walking to my desk.

vote .

eight

----

2 □□□ □□□□□

"Good Afternoon everyone" I spoke walking into the department with my cup of coffee clocking in.

"Good Afternoon" everyone else responded back with a little smile.

Matt told me that James did give him a location which is good. So today we would be heading there.

"Baptise we have another case" Matt told me.

"Damn let me sit down first" I said in my head

"Okay let's go"—"How is the family" She asked Matt as they walked towards the scene.

"They doing okay" Matt slightly shrugged his shoulders.

"Oh"

" Detective Day, Do you know what happened here?" I asked putting on some gloves walking around the scene.

"It looks like the victim was trying to rob the store clerk and failed,he was taken down to headquarters..but it seems like this was just self defense"

"The victim was shoot once in the right upper quadrant with a 9MM handgun" The weaponologist spoked.

"Did the victim have a gun"

"Yes he did" The weaponologist replied walking over towards the evidence bags.

"He had a AR-15 rifle"

"That big ass gun for a store robbery" I mumbled.

"How many casings was found" I asked trying to see if the victim let off any shots.

"Only 4 it's looks like" She replied

"Any surveillance footage" I turned around and asked Detective Day.

"Yeah all from different angles" She replied

"Matt and I are about to go continue our other case..stay safe" I told her

"Same too you"—"Have you ever been over this way" I asked Matt as we drove to the destination that was giving by James.

"No have you"

"I rarely leave the house so no" I replied looking out the window at the beautiful trees and children that was running around in they front yard playing.

Kids are adorable.

"We are here" He spoke as he pulled the eyes out of the ignition.

I unbuckled my seatbelt looking around taking in everything.

As Matt steps out the car he walks towards a single 1 story house that looks to be abandoned. I followed behind him as he walked towards the front door.

"Dont we need a warrant" He looks back and asked me.

"No" I shrugged my shoulders as I walked infront of him.

I twist the doorknob not thinking it's going to open.As soon as I opened the door,I was hit with a strong smell of chemicals.I covered my nose with my arm as we continue to walk further into the house

The house had little to no furniture. The crazy thing was that it looks like someone was cleaning it,well attempted to clean it.

I walked towards what looks like the living room and see a single chair in the middle of the floor.

"This is where they must have kept Monica" She told Matt as she walked towards the chair.

"They"

"Yes they, he said he didn't do it and whoever he was working for did it"I turned around and looked at Matt.

"I kinda want to believe him you know"I shrugged my shoulders as I kept walking around.

"The fuck is that"Matt asked smelling the top of the 100 lb Empty Steel Cylinder Tank.

"Acetylene, Propane?"

"No,Ammonia" I responded

even if youu dont comment youu can vote .

nine

THURSDAY

"What the actual fuck did James get himself into" I asked putting the tank down going towards the other side of the the room.

"We need to get a Chem transport team and a CSI out here right now Matt"

"Im on it" He responded pulling his phone out his pocket.

On the other side of the room was a table full of weapons....torture weapons. I didn't want to touch anything to destroy any evidence. So I looked but didn't touch.

"Matt" I called out for him but he didn't respond.

"MATT !!" I called once again and this time he showed up coming out the dining room way.

"Did you call them"

"Yeah Yeah I did..I can stay here til they should up, you can leave"

"Why I gotta always leave" I responded walking towards the exit.

"I dont have to explain myself Nayla" He looked at me like he really wasn't about to explain his-self.

"How i'm going to leave though we drove together" I wiggled my eyebrows at him.

"Once they show up I will drop you off at headquarters and come back" He gave me that ugly as evil smirk.

"Fuck you" I put up my middle finger.

—

"Next time i'm not leaving" I told him as I got out the car and walked into headquarters.

It's currently 7 and I have nothing to do but go home,I really dont want to go home so Ima go to my parents house.

I straighten up around my desk making sure i'm not leaving nothing behind. I get up and say my goodbyes to everyone who was there and clocked out.

Once my ass touched my car seat I let out a sigh because why it's soo damn hot. I have a black 2021 Jeep Wrangler with 15% tint with trim pink custom interior.

I put my key in the ignition connecting my phone to the radio. I turned on the air as I scrolled through my play list finding some to play.

"Maybe I should go home and feed Dino and take a shower while i'm there" I said to myself

I decided to play □□□□□□ □□ □□□

Need you for the old me Need you for my sanityNeed you to remind me where I come from

I sung before I pulled off

—"Dino" I called out

I hear him panting as he runs towards me.

"How was your day..huh" I rubbed behind his ear as he closed his eyes enjoying the feeling.

"You want a treat...huh..you want a treat"

I walked into the kitchen opening the bottom cabinet where I keep his things at.

"You do a trick for me I will give you a treat" I waved a dog treat in-front of his face as I wait for him.

He starts standing on his hind legs walking towards me.

"Good boy" I smiled giving him his treat

"Can mommy record you stink" I asked pulling out my phone like he's going to really care.

□□□□.□□□□□□□□□□

Liked by □□□□□□□□□□□ and 13,230 others □□□□.□□□□□□□□□□□: Live,Laugh,Bark View all 10,431 comments □□□□□□□□□□□: My Son . —

"Im going to feed you than take a shower" I told him as I headed to the kitchen to get his food.

"I might take you with me"

vote . comment .

ten

A pril 2022

"Mari get up mane" Tay come in and snatched the covers off of me.I mugged the hell out of him because what are you doing.

"□□□ □ □□□□□ □□ □□ □□□□□ □□ □ □□□□ □□□□ □□ □□□" I signed to him as I get up and head into the bathroom brushing my teeth.

"Today is Friday stop being like that" He yelled from the other side of the door as I started taking my clothes off getting into the shower.

"Do it seems like I give a damn what day it is" I mumbled to myself.

"I'm going to go fix breakfast, you actually got up this time" He told me as I could barely hear him as washed my face looking confused asf.

"WHAT !!" I screamed back

"I said IM GOING TO GO FIX BREAKFAST" He yelled back.

"Okay" mumbled grabbing my other rag to wash my body.

"WAIT WHAT TIME IS IT" I yelled back making sure he hear me

"It's 6:30" He responded laughing on the other side of the door.

I didn't find shit funny at all why am I up this damn early nothing is funny.

"Get out mane shit ain't even funny" I responded washing my body off making sure my dick clean as well.—

"What you even cooking" I asked sitting on the counter rubbing my ear as I watching him fixing some shit. I actually know how to cook I just never wake up early enough to actually cook and around dinner time we just eat out.

"Food...Where is your hearing aid" He asked me while I continued to rubbed over my left ear.

"I-I umm broke it" I stumbled over my words trying to lie but I know he doesn't believe me.He looks at me suspicious.

"What do you mean you broke it" He asked turned the stove off putting the food on the plates.

"I stepped on it by a-accident that's all" I shrugged my shoulders getting off the counter walking towards a plate. I mean I did step on it so im not actually really lying.

"Yeah whatever I dont believe it" He responded getting his food and sitting down.

"Wont be home again today..Be safe going home"He told me while he ate his food.

"Okay well...its 7:36,Can you take my pic once we done?" I asked him as I basically inhaled my food.

"Yeah"—

□□.□□□□□□□□□

Liked by □□□.□□□ and 1,230 others □□.□□□□□□□□□:View all 800 comments □□□.□□□: Brother . —Same thing as everyday, get pat down and goes through the metal detector. Students still in the hall as I faintly hear the bell go off. I honestly can't wait til im out of here.

Ms.Ray still doesn't know when to hush.Been talking about how bad traffic was and shit, knowing nobody cares.

"Back in my day I-" she couldn't even finish her sentence because the bell had rung telling us it's time to head into 2nd period.

I got up so damn fast even though I cant hear out of my left ear I can still hear out of my right ear.

I head into 2nd period sitting in the front so I can get out the class faster.

Mr.Reed was here today surprisingly. He was a cool as Math teacher but this man is never at work,that's not my business.

Zamari had his head laying on his desk but once he heard Mr.Reed calculation the whole equation wrong he sat up.

"That's wrong" I announced getting yo from my seat walking towards the board. I erased everything and did it over. From the corner of my eye I can see him looking at me.

"See try it the other way it adds up to 365..Only 1 answer can be correct" I told him putting down the expo marker. He looked at my fire in his eyes, I wasn't trying to embarrass him or anything.

"I-Im sorry,I dont mean any disrespect but your c-calculations are wrong" I stuttered as I pulled at the skin on my hand. Everyone was looking at me and that was making me nervous,so I just went back to sleep and layed my head down.

vote. comment .

eleven

It's the end of the day and I have to walk home by myself.Not saying that im scared or anything but damn I really have to walk.

"You think you smart huh?"The same dude that took my hearing aid spoke.

I just kept walking towards the exit of the school. I will really fuck this dude up but i'm trying to keep calm.

"I want some peanut butter" I random spoke to myself as he kept talking shit behind me.

"Yo pussy ass" He muttered as he pushed me out the door almost causing me to fall.

At first I wasn't going to do nothing but I really want some peanut butter so I just hit his ass one good time and kept walking.

The Circle K should have a jar of peanut butter and if they dont i'm going to be pissed asf because I walked all this way for nothing.

"Lolli, lolli" I mumbled pulling open the door walking towards the counter.

"Aye yah selling peanut butter" I asked the clerk who wasn't paying attention to me all.So I hit the glass hard asf not caring if it broke because I know he hear me.

I started rubbing my ear because it started to buzz from me hitting the glass so hard.

"Yah selling peanut butter or what mane" I asked getting irritated.

He still wasn't answering so I walked around the store looking for the peanut butter. Took me a couple of minutes because I kept getting off track looking at icecream and shit knowing I didn't come in here for that.

"Finally" I mumbled to myself picking up the Pintola All Natural Peanut Butter.

I walked over to the food station pick up a spoon.I walked towards the beverage aisle and picked up a peach lemonade. I love me some Peach lemonade boaaaa.

"You gon ring this up or I can walk straight out this bitch" I ask him as I put my items on the counter waiting for him to ring it up.

"$2.79" He spoke with a attitude like I wont walk out this store right now.

"Gimmie my damn change" I muttered snatching it out his hand stick it in my pocket.

I cant wait to eat this,I can just feel my mouth watering just thinking about it.

"Lolli, lolli, lolli, lolli, lolli..I'm a lil wicked nigga" I muttered as I walked down the sidewalk heading home with my peanut butter and lemonade in my hand happy asff.

As im walking I hear voices in the alley and you know i'm black asf sooooo I went towards the alley hiding behind the wall. I put my things down making sure i'm careful ain't trying to get caught.

I put my right ear out towards the voices so I can hear a little better.

"Maybe I should leave" I tell myself because if I get caught im dead for sure but I become im nosey.

I stick my head out and I see 2 guys. One has his back towards me and let me say this dude big ash. What could he possibly be eating his big ass.

I know a little something bout languages so I know one is speaking Italian and the other is speaking Mandarin I think.

They get to discussing about drugs some words are spoken in english so I understand what they saying. I decided I've heard enough but once I started to get up I see Tay.

"Tay" I whispered in shock.

twelve

"Tay" I whispered in shock.

Is this why he's always coming home late. I kinda scund like a wife that's getting cheating on but that's not the point.

"Una volta che ha dato questo pezzo di carta, nulla dovrebbe essere condiviso qui,Do you understand me? The Italian guy spoke giving me the other guy the piece of paper.

"Yeah I understand" he responded putting the paper in his pocket

"Good, It was great making this deal with you"

Once I seen they was heading my way I hurried up and grabbed my things running back towards the store. I realized I wasn't going tc make it I just turned into another damn alley.

"This is all types of fucked up" I muttered bout tired ash.

I stood in the alley for a few minutes just talking to myself making sure they are really gone. I leaned my head out a little and seen them leaning on the car smoking.

" If they dont hurry up mane, Im literally in a damn alley someone can come snatch my luh ass up" I complained pacing back and forth

A couple of minutes later I hear some doors shut and a car pull off.

"God damn finally" I sighed

As I walked down out the alley with a now warm ass bottle of lemonade and a jar of peanut butter that's probably melting, I see a piece of paper. I thought it was money sooo youu know I picked it up.

"What is this" I asked myself putting my lemonade under my arm once I realized it wasn't money.I opened the paper and seen just number written all over it.

I knew they wasn't just random numbers they had to have some type of pattern.

Once it clicked that this is the paper they was talking about. I put that motherfucker in the nearest trashcan I found and ran my monkey ass home.

vote . comment .

thirteen

"HER FINGER OMG" Zamari semi-yelled watching the movie "Hush" while eating strawberry shortcake icecream on this Saturday afternoon.

"Why are youu screaming man" Tay walked down the stairs rubbing his eyes, indicating he just woke up.

"My fault but it's 7:00 pm why you still sleep?" I asked pausing the movies turning around on the couch.

Tay just looked at Zamari blankly,He just woke up and could barely comprehend what he was saying. Tay didn't even know what was really going on.

"Huh" Tay replied still standing at the foot of the stairs.

"Why you just standing right there" Zamari laughed as Tay just stood there looking like a whole Summer Walker meme.

"Nahh but fr though ah nigga starving"

"Go cook den nigga ain't yo maid" Tay replied walking back upstairs heading into the bathroom.

Zamari stood up walking into the kitchen putting the icecream up and throwing the plastic spoon away.

He walked upstairs seeing Tay in his room laying on his back with his phone in his hand."Ima head to Circle K and get some pizza or some shii, you want some" Zamari asked standing in the entrance of the room.

"Nah i'm straight, the key downstairs on the counter" Tay replied sitting up reaching for the game controller.

"When I come back with some you want dont ask for shit because I asked you before I left" Zamari told him already knowing as soon as Tay see that he got some he going to ask for it.

"I'm not stop acting like you know me" Tay chuckled picking up the headset putting it on.—Just got a lil one smoked, gun shotJust got a new chop, one smoke, get poppedLil Wick with the shit, dirty soul like a sock.

Mari has been writing down shit that was coming to his mind lately. He wasn't so sure about the making music but Tay always told him he had this shit in the bag and he could go far with this shit.

Zamari put his hands in his hood as he walked with his head trying to hurry up and head to the store.

As he continued walking he seen a pair of shoes stopped in-front of him. He kept his head down trying to walk around the person, but every time he would move they would also move

"Can you move out the way mane, I'm hungry asff right about now" Zamari expressed.

"You have something I need" The guy spoke in a heavy Mandarin accent.

Zamari had a clue what he was talking about but he didn't want act suspicious so he just acted normal.

"You dont even know me" Zamari walked around him this time continuing his journey to the store.

He grabbed Zamari upper arm turning him around."The paper with some numbers on it, Where is it?" He asked keeping his grip on his arm.

Zamari yanked his arm out his grip with a mug on his face. " I dont know what your talking about, Now leave me alone"

"We know everything about okay, We know you have the number just give it back" He replied stepping back rubbing his eyebrow.

" Or we could just simply take you and torture you till you give it up"

"I dont know what your talking about man" Zamari rubbed his stomach as it growled

The guy was getting irritated because he needed the number or else HE will kill him.

He spoke in his native tongue calling other guys over to pull Zamari in his car for him.

Zamari didnt know if he should run or run, because he was gon run anyways. He didn't want to get tortured.

So he ran thinking about the good ass food he could have possible got from Circle K.

fourteen

Zamari had been for minutes now just turning corners, he knew his way around the Detroit so finding abandoned houses to hide in was easy for him.

"Where could his little ass go" One of the 5 guys spoke.

Zamari had to cover his mouth so he wouldn't laugh because why did they have to do him like that.

"He a little fast motherfucker"

They began searching for Zamari trashing the already trash house. Opening all the room doors flipping all the dusty furniture

"□□□□" The one who grabbed me earlier spoke pulling at his hair. (Where is he)

Zamari legs was starting to hurt because he bending behind the refrigerator side ways, as he was moving around trying to release the pain he heard the door open.

Thinking that they left he stayed there for a more seconds til he heard and Italian accent.

"I thought boss told you not to lose the number Chang Quan?" A heavy Italian accent spoke,"We need them numbers to be coded".

Zamari stayed behind the refrigerator trying to stay still,his knees felt like they was locked.Mari tried to rearrange his-self but he hit his knee which caused a loud thump.

"Welp they found me" He muttered getting from behind the refrigerator stretching his legs.

All they guys looked towards him with anger,confusion or both .

"He know where the code is"Change replied point to Zamari

The Italian guy and his team looked confused as ever.

"How many times im gon tell you I dont" Zamari corrected him as he tried to wipe the dust off his pants as he stood behind one of the guys.

"Im done playing game with you Chang, you had one job and you fucked up." He told Chang as he pulled out a gun off his waist.

Zamari started looking around for another exit,they was in the kitchen and he wasn't going to make it towards the back door.

He knew this wasn't going to end well because now everyone had guns pointing at eachother and he didn't want to be in the middle of it.

"Can we all just ta-"

Zamari couldn't finish his sentence before the guy infront him got shot in the head causing his blood to fall on Zamari face.

Shots start ringing out causing his ears to ring loudly as he ran towards the living room hoping the door was going to open.

"Great" He muttered once he pulled at the handle to find the door jammed.

"TROVA QUEL BASTARDO,AL LLAMAR A LOS DEMÁS " The Italian guy spoke.(Find that bastard,I'm calling the others)

Zamari was now scared. His ears are ringing, he's in the middle of a gun fight he can't find a damn exit and he has a dead person blood on him.

"Please lord help me" He silently prayed over and over again.

The next best thing was a window,he had to try something.

Zamari picked up a lamp that was in corner of the room and started hit the window trying to at least crack it. After a few more hits the window broke causing the glass to go everywhere.

"Shit" He muttered dropping the lamp down fast hopping through the window. Zamari upper half was through the window before someone pulled his leg causing him to fall on the broken glass.

Zamari groaned feeling the glass pierced through his hand as he tried to stop himself from falling.

"Ora devo ucciderti perché hai il codice e stai cercando di scappare" The Italian evilly smiled at Zamari as he picked up his gun.(Now I have to kill you because you have the code and trying to escape)

Zamari didnt want to die today all he wanted was some food from Circle K that's all. So he kicked the man in his face with his size 10 white forces hard asf making the man dropped his gun holding his face he yelled in pain.

Zamari had to make sure he wasn't going to stop him again so he picked up the gun pointing it at him.

"You dont know how to use a gun kid" The guy chuckled with a now dislocated nose. Zamari just smiled at him putting the gun in his right hand because his left hand had glass pierced through his skin.

Zamari is left handed.

He pulled the slide back with his thumb and forefinger before shooting him in the leg before hopping out the window.

Zamari was drained, with all that he been through he was still hungry. Running on a empty stomach, dirty,ear ringing and he still had the glass in his left hand.

When he figured he was good to stop running he pulled the glass out with a groan. Instead of feeling pain he felt pleasure, this blood was making him hard right about now.

This was definitely not the right time to be hard.

Zamari pulled out his phone seeing it was going on 10 o'clock and his phone was going dead.He was going through his contacts to call Tay before his phone go dead.

He heard the same Italian voice which caused him to put his phone in his pocket,holding his hand in his chest as he began running.

Zamari just wanted to cry his eyes out.

He jumped over a fence as best as he could with 1 hand

There was a sliding double door slightly opened.

" They must be white as hell" He thought

This was a nice house in one of da nicer neighborhood's.

Once he made it inside he closed and locked the doors slightly backing up still holding his hand that was bleeding.

Zamari slowly started walking towards the room becoming dizzying from all the blood he lost.

"F-Fuck" He muttered before he passed out in the strangers living room.

the longest chapter ii wrote so far,990 words .

vote . comment .

fifteen

- -

MOMENTS BEFORE .

"GOODMORNING USAAA" Nayla screamed while she had a towel wrapped around her body as she air dried.

That theme song has been in her head all day.

It's 3:20 pm on a Saturday and Nayla figured since she's off today she could go to the mall and shop a little.

"Dino baby wake up" Nayla tried wake up the cavapoo who was in her bed sleeping like he has 2 jobs

□□□□□□□□□□□

Liked by □□□□□__ and 23,870 others □□□□□□□□□□□: Son sleeping like he has a job .View all 13,467 comments □□□: look at the stuffed animal □ □ □□□□□□□□□: Dino □□□□□□□□□□□□□: Leave him alone and bring him over here———Nayla laughed looking at her mom comment. She's starting to feel like her persons love her dog more than her.

Nayla held on to towel searching for something to wear as she hummed a random song.

Since it was a little sunny out Nayla decided she should wear a sun dress with her some sandals, her toes was painted white while her nails where a light pink color.

They were short because of her work.

Nayla went into the bathroom looking in the mirror trying to figure out what to do with her hair.

30 minutes later she just decided to keep it down. Every style she tried wasn't working for her and she started to get frustrated.

Cried a little but that's not the point.

"Come on baby" Nayla spoke picking up Dino like he was a baby. Dino is like a whole baby and he's he's only 1.

Nayla loved kids and hope one day she can have a few of her own ofc with the right person.

Nayla grabbed her some snacks out the cabinet putting them in her purse and a cold bottle of water out the refrigerator while trying to hold Dino up as he continued to sleep.

She didn't need to get anything for him because he literally had everything at her parents house so he was straight.

"It's so hot out here" She spoke as she stepped out the door locking her house up,walking towards her Jeep putting him on the passenger seat.

She closed the door walking to the passenger side, immediately putting her keys in the ignition turning on some air.

"This sun though" Nayla mumbled pulling out her phone getting on the camera app. The sun wasn't playing today .

□□□□□□□□□□

Liked by □□□□□□□□□□□□ and 70,356 others □□□□□□□□□□□□: All natural .View all 40,436 comments □□□□□□□□□□□□□□:Mi hermosa hija.

—"Volveré más tarde hoy, ¿vale?"(I will be back later on today okay) Nayla spoke to her mama who was standing in the doorway holding Dino.

Katherine didn't mind at all if her daughter wanted her to watch Dino. Her husband was always at work, he was a neurologist. Michael was always a busy man which Katherine knew.

Katherine was lonely sometimes being that she is a piano pedagogues, that was her part-time job.She would teach kids 7-13 private lessons at her home.

One day she wish to have grandchildren but surely isn't rushing her daughter so Dino would do just fine.

Meanwhile,Nayla was starting to think something was wrong with her dog, because there's no way he's always sleeping or maybe he's just a lazy ass dog.

...Dino is a lazy ass dog.

"Adiós a esta chica" Katherine spoke rocking Dino side to side as continued to sleep. ("I got this girl bye").

"okay okay" Nayla responded putting her car in drive. She was just always worried about him all the times every though she trust her parents.

Before Nayla could pull off she gets a phone call from Detective Day, She wasn't going to answer because it's her day off but she did anyways.

"Hello" Nayla answered waving at her mom who was going back into the house.

"We need you at headquarters like right now"

sixteen

"We need you at headquarters like right now" Detective Day spoke through the phone in a very serious voice.

"I-Um Okay what happened" I asked putting my car in park before I get to damn rolling.

"Just come down here it's...crazy" she spoke with a sigh at the end sounding irritated.

"Okay..Im on the way" Nayla told her hanging up the phone.

So much for a off day. ✸✸✸Before she headed towards headquarters she went home to change her clothes and put her hair in a messy bun.

Walking inside the department she see literally every one running around with like a chicken with they head cut off.

"What is going on" She thought to herself clocking in. Just because it's an off day doesn't mean she's not gonna clock in.

"Hey Maddie what's going on" She asked calling Detective Day by her real name.

Maddie was at her desk with files everywhere.

" You want the bad news or...bad news" She responded looking up at Nayla who had a confused look on her face.

"Bad new" Nayla shrugged with a sigh, she really didn't have a choice they both was bad news.

"Um you remember James right aka G-Baby" Maddie asked putting her file down getting ready to deliver all the shit that's been going on today.

"Yeah how could I forget" Nayla responded pulling up a chair next to her desk.

"Some how in his jail cell he was exposed to some synthetic chemical compounds, the ones that was in the CSI report that you found."

Nayla remember the chemicals she found in the abandoned house that G-Baby gave them the location to.

"They had to put him in a drug-induced coma, to try and slow down the process."

At this moment Nayla is lost for words, how could this happen in a damn jail cell where was the security.

"His body is temperature has been lowered significantly, Nobody hasn't seen anything like this before and the C.D.C has sent in specialist.

"The substance that's affecting him, they haven't been able to identify or any additional contaminants."

"This is so wild...On my day off though" She mumbled shaking her head. "What's the other bad news"

"You probably have to move your seating just a for a little while youu see all theses people"

Nayla mugged Maddie because she didn't wanna leave her damn seat, she been there every since she join.

"Why the f-" Nayla couldn't finish her sentence because her boss had walked into headquarters giving everyone news they didn't want to hear.

"THE REAPER HAS STRIKES AGAIN...I NEED EVERYONE ON SCENE, THIS ONE IS MESSY"

This caused everyone to goes silent. The Reaper hasn't caused any crime in almost a year and when he did it was gruesome.

✖✖✖

Arriving at the scene it's total chaos, screaming filled Nayla ears with red and blue flashing lights in-front of her and the other Detectives eyes.

Nayla ducked under the yellow tape following behind her boss heading into the house. The abandoned house had blood and bodies everywhere. Blood leaking down the wall and pools of blood on the floor.

A lot of shell casings on the floor and bullet holes in the wall.

This was definitely gang related.

This was another one of Reaper crimes, this person has been committing crimes way before Nayla had join the team. They never had any leads on who it was.

"This one is going to be a crazy one" Nayla mumbled putting on her gloves and things to cover her shoes.

seventeen

I t was now 2 in the morning when Nayla finally clocked out. She was ready to go home to take a mean ass hot shower and probably eat something.

Her and the team been going over all the evidence that they tried ta find at the crime.There was nothing to go one really, nothing but bodies, guns and blood.

The evidence has been sent to the evidence lab so when or IF any results come in I will get a call.

Hopefully I get a call.

On the way home Nayla was just think about her little puppy and how much she misses him.

It's midnight so she will get him in the morning, she didn't want to wake up her parents just to get him.

"I'm not going in tomorrow I hope they know that" Nayla spoke to herself as put her car in parked turning off the engine.

Nayla made sure she had everything in her purse and getting her keys to the house.

She got out the the car locking the doors in the process unlocking her door humming to □□□□□ □□ □□□□□□ □□□□□□□

Nayla pushed the door open taking her shoes off leaving them by the door. She put her purse on the entryway table leaving her gun on her waist.

As she was walking towards the living room to turn the lamp on her she's a silhouette of someone on the floor.

The house was dark but the street lights was on which gave the house just some like.

"I-Wait" Nayla stuttered trying to process what's going on. She didn't know if she should be scared or what.

Nayla careful walked towards the lamp to turn it on so she could she whoever this person was on her damn floor.

She twist the lamp switch around twice as her hand was on her gun,When the light flicked on she could see a skinny boy who looks like he's been through hell.

His face had dried up blood his hand was on his chest that looks like to be hurt.

Nayla thought that the homeless person just made a mistake and stumbled in her house but she seen the clothes and shoes he had on he couldn't be homeless.

"Soo there is someone laying on my floor who could possibly kill me once they wake u-" Nayla stopped midway through her sentence walking closer to see if he was breathing.

Buddy was laid out on the floor like he was dead.

She moved a little closer kicking him in his shoulder getting a small groan from him.

"I'm sorry..I'm soo sorry omg." Nayla apologize softly starting to freak out. "He's not dead so that's good"She breaths out relaxing just a little, still freaking out.

She knelt down beside his head getting a better view of him.

He was brown-skin with some big ass ears, his eye shape was small, he had brown eyes, and his nose was big but his lips was full and 2 toned so it evened out his whole face.

He was truly handsome.

"What happened to you" Nayla whispered as she grabbed him by his shoulder leaning him up again the couch.

Just doing that had her tired asf.

"This is going to take a while aint it". Nayla breathe out questioning herself.

my man so fine yah.

any mistakes lmk. couldn't proofread fr because this Spanish teacher is watching my ass like a hawk.

eighteen

M ay 2020

"Never a fucking again never" Nayla spoke tired as hell.

Nayla had to try to carry his heavy ass up the stairs as best as she could. He might be skinny but that boy was holding weight.

She had to carry his ass to the guest bedroom so she could can clean him up just a little. He wasn't stinky but still he was dirty.

She just gave him a wash-up because she didn't want to invade his privacy.

Nayla washed his face and changed his clothes leaving him in his boxers. She had a big shirt that she sometimes sleep in that could be big enough for him but she didn't have any bottoms so he was just left in his underwear.

Hoping she wasn't really invading his privacy.

When she finally got him cleaned she put him in the bed tucking him in.

Nayla had to stop herself from rubbing over his lips that's was slightly pouted.

"I wonder how he hasn't woke up yet with all that movement" Nayla thought to herself slowly rubbing over his eyebrows.

" Hurry up and wake up so you can get the hell out my house" She whispered laughing at herself as she walked towards her bathroom.
✴✴✴"Mamá" Nayla spoke to her mother over the phone while she was in the kitchen cooking breakfast.

"Hoy no podré asistir a la iglesia, ha surgido algo.(I won't be able to attend church today something has came up.)

Even though her mother wasn't Columbian she still knew how to speak Spanish.

"¿Por qué no es el primer domingo?" (Why not it's First Sunday) Katherine spoke through the phone as she walked towards the church locking arms with her husband.

Dream City Church isn't very pet friend so Katherine had to leave Dino at home all by himself.

He's probably going to sleep til church is over so that's okay.

"Something has came up today but I promise i'm going next Sunday" Nayla told her mom as she plated the food on separated plates.

The guy was probably going to be hungry ,She didn't know how long he was there on her living room floor so Nayla cooked enough for them both of them.

"Okay just tell me what's going on whenever you ready okay."

"Yes I will" Nayla smiled just thinking about the good relationship she has with her parents.

"Your dad and I are heading into church now te queremos lala." (We love you)

Katherine would always let her Daughter and Husband know she loves them every hour and every minute,Life is crazy now days.

" I love you guys more...have a great service and pray for me" Nayla told her Mother hanging up putting they food in the microwave that was big enough for both plates.

Nayla went upstairs to see if the guy was woke yet. She checked up on him when she woke up and that was at 5 in the morning. He been sleep all day, haven't even moved once to change his sleep position.

She pushed open the guest bed room and see that he was still in the same sleeping position but his facial expression had changed.

At first he was pouting like he was sad or hurting but now he just looked relaxed and calm.

That was good.

Nayla was hoping that once he woke up he wasn't a crazy man that wanted to rob her or something because she might have to kill him,even she didn't want to kill the handsome guy.

She walked towards the pulling out some Carmex out the nightstand putting some on his lips. His lips was getting dry so she figured he was dehydrated.

Once she was done applying Carmex on his lips she put it back in the night stand walking back towards the door heading downstairs to get him something to drink.

"If he dont wake up soon I might have to call the ambulance" She thought to herself grabbing a cold bottle out the refrigerator walking back to the guest bedroom.

She was starting to worry about him, that was the Detective in her wanting to investigate what happened to him.

As soon as she open the door she meet with a pair of brown eyes.

He was looking into her eyes for a little while before looking down at his hands. Eye contact made him nervous.

i'm soo tired rn but no matter how tired i am i'm never going ta sleep in class.

nineteen

Zamari sat up breathing heavy rubbing his eyes trying to calm down from the nightmare he just had.

As he continues to calm down his breath he realized he wasn't in his roo m...let alone his house. He was trying to recall everything that happened after he passed out.

"Oh lord they got me" He let out a sigh falling back on the bed looking up at the ceiling. This was not a nightmare and everything that occurred really did happen.

Zamari heard light footsteps walking towards the room causing him to sit up a little bit.What he didn't expect was a petite woman with a bottle of water in her hand standing by the doorway looking directly at him.

Her hair was in a messy bun on top of her head she had on a pastel green crop top with grey joggers. Nayla had on her glasses today because she was planning on reading later.

"Hey" Nayla spoke softly walking towards him sitting on the end of the bed.

Zamari just kept playing with his hands scared to talk he knew he was going to stutter because how nervous he was. She was so beautiful to him and looking in her eyes would definitely make him blush.

Nayla handed him water bottle waiting for him to take it. "Your probably thirsty so here is some cold water"

"Huh" He whispered lifting his head up a little to try and hear her better. Seeing that she was holding a bottle of water in her he took the water mumbling a small thanks.

He opened the bottle of water taking a huge gulp that made Nayla eyes widen a little, he was very thirsty.

"I hope you didn't mind.. I washed you up a little bit youu was a little dirty and dont worry I didn't take off your boxers" She told him giving him a nervous smile.

Zamari pulled up the cover looking down at seeing that he was in a shirt that was kinda big on him. He was tall but he was very skinny, with a little muscles.

"T-Thanks again but I-I have to leave" He told her starting to pull the covers down his leg. He didn't know if they had followed him and he didn't want to cause any danger to the beautiful lady that was in front of him.

"Wait- How you get inside here" She asked standing up fixing her glasses that was on her face that was slightly falling off.

"Huh" He asked sitting back down feeling lightheaded grabbing his head,probably because he hasn't ate and his stomach was crying right now for some food.

"Are you okay" Nayla asked moving towards him inspecting his face as he grabbed his head in pain.

"Y-yes just hungry that's all" He replied trying to stand up again but Nayla pushed him down by his shoulders.

"I made breakfast okay it's downstairs" She told him rubbing his shoulder in a soothing manner. "I can go get it for you if you like"

"Y-Yes please" He whispered looking up at Nayla with a pout on his lips as he felt his stomach growling in hunger.

He was so hungry right now and it was embarrassing hearing his stomach growling...loudly.

"Just get back in bed and I will bring it up to you, Do you want some more water or anything" Nayla asked walking towards the door turning around to hear his answer.

"Apple Juice" Mari whispered pulling the covers up on his chin really wanting his stomach to hush. This whole situation was embarrassing.

"I will be back with your food.. I have a spare toothbrush in the bathroom under the cabinet along with some rags and towels" Nayla told him walking out the room heading downstairs.

She grabbed her food out the microwave and leaving his in setting the timer on 30 minutes.Before the timer hit 1 she opened the microwave putting her food back in.

Nayla grabbed a glass cup out of the top cabinet washing it out with hot water and dishwashing liquid.

She poured him some apple juice in the filling it up to the top. Nayla grabbed her food tray sitting his food and drink down on the tray grabbing plastic and silverware just in-case.

"Let's not forget the napkins" She mumbled to her self turning around grabbing a few napkins out the napkin stand.

Careful she picked up the tray making sure she dont waste anyways slowly walking up the 12 stairs.

She pushed opened the door with her foot walking towards him sitting his food down on his lap as he just looked mesmerized by the food on his tray.

"Y-You didn't have to cook all of this I-I could have just got cereal or something" He mumbled playing with his left ear,this shit was starting to irritate Mari.

"Are you okay" Nayla asked she was watches him aggressively rubbing his left ear.

He didn't answer her, he just kept rubbing his ear praying that the buzzing would stop.

Nayla grabbed his hand removing it from his ear, rubbing his ear in a soft manner. Zamari let out a soft sigh as he picked up a piece of bacon as she continued to rub his ear

"Your phone is in my room, I had charged it up for you" Nayla told him removing her hand from his ear.

" We have to talk once your done eating okay" She told him getting up grabbing a napkin cleaning the side of his lip that had a string of cheese from the grits.

Zamari nodded his head felling embarrassed that he had food on the side of his mouth. "Enjoy your food"

twenty

▢ □□□□□ □□□ □□□□ □□□□□ .

"Can I come in" Nayla asked knocking on the guest room door.Even though this was her house she still wanted to be respectful enough to knock.

Zamari jumped a little because he was into the Tv, the sudden voice had scared him.

"Huh" He mumble turning the Tv down trying to hear her better. After a few seconds she didn't responded so he figured she didn't hear him.

Mari walked towards the door opening it seeing the beautiful lady. Nayla hair was messy and she looked tired but in all she's still beautiful.

"Are you okay" Nayla asked him seeing that he was staring at her. She pulled her hair out of her bun thinking that she looked a mess right now,that's why he's probably staring.

"Y-Yeah" He spoke looking down, embarrassed that he got caught staring. Mari couldn't help it ,way did she look so fine it didn't make no damn sense.

"Can we talk downstairs" She asked as she watched him rubbed his ear. Nayla noticed he played with his left ear a lot.

"Yes" He whispered

Nayla also noticed that he doesn't talk a lot and if he did he would always mumble it,maybe he wasn't a talker and that was fine with her.

Nayla give him a little smile getting one in return,she had to hold on her scream because he has dimples.

He has a really pretty smile.

Nayla turned around heading downstairs with a smile on her lips,She cooked dinner for them it was currently 7:00 pm.

Nayla made Sancocho which contains potatoes, yuca, corn, plantains, and chicken.Sancocho will always be her dish to eat, even though it doesn't taste the exact same as her dad it was still good.

She plated both of they plates in the dining room,a glass of Apple Juice for him and a glass of Sweet Tea for her.

Nayla put some napkins on both sides of they plates right alone with either plastic or silver silverware.

Nayla was hoping she wasn't doing too much with how she was treating him,she just wanted him to be comfortable even though he probably won't be here long.

"I made some Sancocho, If you dont like it I can make you something else" She told him realizing that he probably doesn't eat this.

"N-No it's okay, I should just be appreciative thank y-you" He gave her a small smile.

Mari loved how she took care of him even though she dont even know him from a can of paint. He was just really appreciative.

"Theres a half bathroom downstairs where you can go wash your hands" She told him walking towards the stove so she can cover the food up.

Nayla would most likely go back for seconds so she didn't put the food up just yet,plus the food had to cool down first before putting up.

"You ready to pray for the food" She asked him sitting down at the other end of the table.

"Yeah" he whispered looking down at his plate, he haven't had a home cooked meal in a while.

After they prayed over the food they just made a little small talk since Mari wasn't speaking much.

"What's your name" She asked him eating a piece potato.

"Z-Zamari Kross Wallace" He told her eating some chicken.He never heard of Sancocho let alone knew what it was. This was so good so he knew this was something that wasn't American.

"Awww that's soo cute my name is Nayla Esmée-Inès Baptise, I am from Bogota but moved when I was younger when my dad have got a job offer"

"I'm from Jacksonville, I moved down here when I was 10 with my parents" Mari told her sipping the stew from his spoon. This shit was so good.

"How did you end up on my living room floor all hurt and things" Nayla asked cleaning up they dinner off they table.

Mari knew this questions was coming sooner or later, he was already prepared to move out the beautiful women house.

"This is gon be a while" Mari told her getting up washing his hands heading toward the living room as he dry his hands and wipe his mouth.

The whole story took a while because Mari either couldn't stay on track or Nayla always had a question.

any mistakes lmk ightt, ii really want some gawd damn umm powder donuts and peanut butter. !

vote and comment plss.

twenty-one

J uly 2020

"MarMar...Dino" Nayla spoke putting her things on the walk-in table.

After everything Mari told her she was completely sure that he got caught up in the Reapers mess.

I didnt push him to talk about the numbers,we will talk about it when he's ready.

"Yes" He whispered walking into the living room eating a jar of peanut butter with Dino following behind him.

Nayla found him very weird because why is he eating peanut butter...by itself.

Mari had on a black tank top, little chains on his neck with some grey nike shorts, looking all good and shit but that's not the point.

Over the past 2 months Nayla have been working on the Reaper and other cases while Mari has been attending school.

Mari is on break right now.

" Hii baby how was your day with Mari" Nayla spoke to Dino who hasn't ran towards her way yet as he sat beside Mari foot.

Dino been acting like Mari was his damn owner and it was fuck me honestly, he stays under him.

"What you doing on the 4th" She asked him taking the peanut butter from him causing him to mug her " Why you looking at me like that" Nayla laughed while he mugged df out of her.

"Because you seen me eating that-enjoying it actually" He told her trailing behind her licking his lips.

"Anyways sir what you doing for the 4th" Nayla asked again handing him a bottle of water knowing his mouth was bout parched asf. Knowing him he probably been eating it all day.

"Did you feed him yet" She asked Mari as he damn near inhaled the water bottle

"T-Thanks but probably nothing since Tay always out and yes ofc I did" He told her wiping his mouth with the back of his hands.

Every since he pasted out in Nana living room he hasn't spoke to Tay and that was over 2 months ago. Tay hasn't even called or text him so he figured that Tay has no idea of what happened.

Mari was still curious as to why Tay haven't check up on him yet.

"I was wondering if you would like to come over to my parents house on the 4th" She asked him heading towards her bedroom.

"Go Play" she commanded Dino as he took off towards the yard that had a built in pet door.

"Your p-parents" Mari asked sitting on her bed playing with his hands starting to get nervous.

"Hey look it's going to be okay,and you dont have to come if you don't want to"She told him kneeling infront of him holding his hands.

Nayla and Mari has been growing close together as friends,though sometimes they will have they little moments but everything is fine in the friend department.

"I want to go b-but what about they don't like me" He whispered looking down at they joined hands. "They will love you,I promise" She told him looking in his eyes.

"Okay" He told her breathing out trying to calm down.

"I'm going to head into the shower now, are you hungry" She asked him taking off her work shirt leaving her in a tank top.

Nayla breast was coming out the top of her just a little so Mari had to look over towards the door knowing that he was blushing.

Didn't needed a genius to know he was a virgin.

"Im not hungry Nana" He told her trying to cover up his boner.

"I'm still going to cook something it's 5:13 right now so" Nayla had this fixed schedule that at every night at 7:00 is dinner time.

"Ok can I umm c-come in there with you" Mari asked her while he was still turnt towards the door.

He wouldn't say he had separation anxiety but he had separation anxiety, and with Nayla being the only person he's been with for the past 2 months he always wanted to be by her.

"Yeah just let me go in first and I will call youu okay" She told him grabbing a towel.

Since she has another person in the house she just can't be walking around naked like she use to do. Definitely wasn't trying to make him uncomfortable.

As Nayla went into the bathroom Mari had put his hand in his boxers wrapping his hands around his dick slightly moaning in the process trying to release the pressure.

"Mar-" Nayla stopped mid sentence seeing Mari back towards her.

At the sound of her voice he hurry up and pulled his hands out his pants turning around with a nervous pout on his lips.

"Y-yes" He stuttered putting his hands in-front of his pants trying to cover up his boner.

"Move your hand baby" She told him walking into the bathroom turning off the water.

"Why" He told her sitting down on the bed with one of her pillows on his lap.

"Because i'm going to help you" Nayla told him dropping her towel in-front of him revealing her perfect body.

at first i was gon wait til they did anything sexual but i'm like fuck it.

twenty-two

D amn...That's all Mari could say.

Standing infront of him was literally a goddess,he have seen naked women before but Nayla was different.

Nayla have big titties that sat up just right with light brown nipples. He can just imagine his mouth wrapped around her nipples and light brown pussy looked so smooth.

"Deja de mirarme así, me pones nervioso"Nayla whispered walking toward him removing the pillow sitting on his lap.("Stop looking at me like that you make me nervous)

Mari released a soft moan feeling her warm pussy on top of clothed dick. "Mami" He whispered in a daze not knowing what he was saying.

"I-I am sorry" He apologize looking down realizing what he just said. " It's okay I like it" Nayla told him holding his head up giving him a kiss on his lips.

This was they first kiss.

"Mhmm more" He whispered carefully putting his hands on her waist not knowing what to do with his hands.

Nayla held his head up holding his neck kissing him more aggressively grinding on his dick.

"Como baby take your clothes off" She told him pulling his shirt off as she got off his lap.

"We can stop if your not comfortable" She told him realizing he was pulling his shorts down slowly.

"N-No I want this...it's just my first time" He whispered.

He didn't know if she wouldn't want him because he was a virgin, he really wanted this to happen with her.

" We can go slow bebé okay" She whispered rubbing his lips that was starting to swell up.

"Okay b-but what if I dont want slow" He told asked rubbing her waist scared to put his hands anywhere else.

"Just tell me okay" She told him grabbing his dick out his boxer rubbing over his tip.

The pleasure felt so good he laid his head on Nayla shoulder wanting to bite her.

"O-Oh okay" He stuttered breathless. "Sit on the bed" She told him, pulling down his boxers off throwing them across the room.

He sat on the edge of the bed grabbing his dick that was slightly harden with every second passing.

"It's so pretty" Nayla told him as she grabbed his now hard dick that was curving downward a little.

"T-thank you" he breathe out

Nayla wrapped one of her arms around his neck as she sat in his lap,Mari slightly moan as Nayla slid her tongue in his mouth holding his neck with her other hand.

"Fuck mhmm" He moaned grabbing my ass, sliding his finger close to her pussy in the process.

Nayla started grinding on his dick making Mari bite her lip just a little.

"Ohh fuck" Nayla moaned feeling Mari dick sliding between her pussy lips. " Nana put it in" Mari told her rocking her hips back and forth a little faster.

"No...not yet" Nayla told him breaking off the kiss letting her spit drop on his dick as she got off his lap.

She got down on her knees putting his tip to her mouth giving him small kisses.

Mari breathing started to pick up when Nayla started places kissing all down his dick til she touched his balls.

Nayla lift his dick up as she put his balls in her mouth just loving the way he taste. "You like that baby" She asked Mari as he just started at her with a lazy smile.

"Yes" He breathe out playing in her hair that was out now out the bun.

As Nayla sucked on his balls she put her hand up to Mari mouth. "Spit" She commanded him and like a good little boy that he is,he did.

Nayla took Mari spit to dick as she started to slide her hand up and down his dick as she continued to suck on his balls.

"That feels really good" Mari moaned throwing his head back. He never knew pleasure like this existed and if Nayla think she gon give him some good shit like this den leave she was tripping.

Nayla ran her tongue up his dick til she got to the top where she started to lightly suck on his tip.

Nayla wrapped her hands around his dick as she took him down her throat relaxing her throat as she looked in his eyes.

Nayla could feel some of his cum going down her throat as she pushed her tongue of forward pushing his dick down her throat more.

"You taste so good" Nayla slightly moaned as she place kissing on his tip that was leaking with his cum.

"Yeah" He mumbled putting both of his hands on the side of Nayla head slowly pushing his dick in and out of her mouth.

"Yes just like that" He moaned feeling his dick touch places he didn't know exist.

Just the feeling of having his dick down her throat made him tighten his hands around her head.

Pounding his dick down her throat making Nayla to gag loudly with tears down her eyes, pushing him away.

"Open" He commanded taping his dick on her lips as she tried to catch her breathe.

The tip of his dick slid right past her lips and into her throat, Nayla held him there with watering eyes. It felts good knowing that Mari was the one doing this to her.

Zamari let out a moan throwing his head back try to catch his breathe. Her mouth was so warm and wet this feeling was forever amazing.

Mari grabbed her neck feeling his dick move in and out her throat moaning at the scene in-front of him.

Nayla was looking so fucking good on her knees with messy hair and tears falling from her red face. This was a sight he would always love to see.

Nayla put both of her hands on his thigh trying to keep herself up felling her stomach knot up. Hearing his moans and the way he was pounding into her mouth was turning her on.

Nayla moaned out loudly around his dick releasing the knot in her stomach.

"M-Mami did you just cum" He asked her lifting her head up wiping her tears that continued to fall from her eyes.

"Yes I couldn't help it" She told him rubbing her pussy trying to release the throbbing that occurred once again.

"Damn" He moaned putting his dick back down her throat grabbing her head fucking her mouth.

"Keep you mouth open baby" He told Nayla hold her still so his dick could rest in the back of her throat.

Nayla pat his thigh so he could let her up, "Mari" she moaned feeing herself bout to cum again.

.

twenty-three

After what happened with me and Mari 3 days ago he's been under me more now. Not saying that I have a problem with it but I'm starting to think he really have separating anxiety.

"Mari" Nayla mumbled softy rubbing his left ear as he slept with her nipple in his mouth playing with her other one.

When Mari told her about his SSHL and what happened to his hearing aid she been looking for a better one for him.

Good news is she knows his ear size and is getting his custom made.

"Mari get up so we can go phat" Nayla told him moving his head from her nipple trying to wake him up.

Mari wasn't moving so Nayla forcefully moved him back causing him to fall off the bed hitting his head on the floor

Nayla got off the bed seeing that he hasn't got up yet. "Mari get up now" Nayla spoke walking on the other side of the bed.

"MARI" Nayla screamed seeing Mari on the floor seizing. Nayla went towards Mari body cradling his head turning him on his side.

"Cariño, lo siento mucho, Dios mío, Mari" Nayla cried seeing that his eyes was rolling to the back of his as he continued to shake.(Baby Im so sorry oh my god Mari)

Nayla grabbed Mari phone that on the nightstand beside her calling 911.

During the 911 call Nayla could barely get her words out Mari has been seizing for about 2 minutes now and he was starting to choke from the lack of oxygen.

"Please hurry h-he can't breathe" Nayla cries got louder seeing him choke. The dispatcher tries to keep her calm letting her know that the ambulance was at her front door.

"In here" She yelled at the EMTs still holding Mari shaking body.

"Step back please" One of the workers told Nayla as she continues to cry.

"How long has he been seizing" They asked Nayla pulling out everything they will possibly need.

"About 5 minutes now" She told them putting on his hoodie and a pair of his sweats.

"I need benzodiazepine right now "

Once they gave him the benzodiazepine he stopped shaking just looking up at the ceiling. "Hey,If you can hear me squeeze my hand twice" the EMT told Mari trying to see if he was responsive.

"Okay good he is responsive but we will have take him down to Crest Care Hospital, you could ride alone or trail behind us" The EMT told Nayla as they put Mari on a Cot Stretcher.

"I will trail behind you guys Thanks" She told walking towards Mari who was still just looking at the ceiling.

"I never meant to hurt you baby I'm so sorry...I love you" Nayla silently cried kissing his lips repeatedly.

Nayla knew right now wasn't the right time to confess her feelings but the thought of losing him terrified her and she really did love him.

□□ □□□ □□□□□□□□

Nayla has been sitting in the waiting room for hours now, still crying about the mistake that could have possibly took Mari away from her.

"Hello" Nayla answered the family gc facetime call.

Nayla didn't put her face in the camera because she knew she looked a hot mess.

"Why-Nayla what's wrong"Katherine asked hearing Nayla sniffing on the other end of the phone.

Hearing something might be wrong with Nayla Michael stop cleaning and put the rag on his shoulders walking over towards his wife.

"Todo es culpa mía, mamá" Nayla wiped her eyes trying not to cry any-more,every time she think about to Mari on the floor shaking made her want to rip her insides out.(It's all my fault Mama)

"No quería presionarlo tanto, solo quería que se levantara" She cried putting her head in her lap.(I didn't want to put so much pressure on him, I just wanted him to get up)

"Nayla baby calm down tell us what happened" Katherine spoke worry-ingly looking up at her husband who was looking down at her with a soft expression.

Nayla wanted her parents to meet Zamari in a good special way,now they have to find out that she put him in the hospital.

"His name is Zamari and I was going to introduce you guys to him today, b-but we was laying down-" Nayla stopped mid-sentence trying to get her words together knowing she was going to cry again.

"I told him to get up but he wouldn't get up so I-I pushed him off the bed not knowing that he was going to fall on the floor Mama, that wasn't supposed to happen" Nayla sniffed looking into the camera.

"Mio Dio" Katherine muttered looking at her daughter who had red puffy eyes, you could tell she's been crying all day.

"He hit his head on the floor and he started to have a seizure" Nayla told her parents who was looking at her with a worried expression.

Every though they didn't know Mari they still was hopping he was okay.

"This Zamari guy your boyfriend or something" Katherine asked with a smirk.

"Mamá ahora definitivamente no es el momento de hablar de esto" Nayla chuckled a little seeing a doctor walk towards her way. (Mama now is most definitely not the time to be talking about this)

"I will call you guys later I love you guys" She told her parents blowing them a kiss.

"Family of Wallace"

ii started on this at 4 in the morning.

twenty-four

Zamari moved his around the uncomfortable spot trying to figure out where he was,the last thing he remember is falling off the bed.

"Nana" He muttered trying to open his eyes but the brightness in the room caused him to close his eyes back.

"Goodmorning Zamari" He heard a man voice.

"Lights off" He spoke raspy telling the man to turn off the lights so he can open his damn eyes.

"Yes ofc..you can open your eyes now"

Zamari tried opened his eyes again,this time successfully.

"Where am I" He asked the male doctor grabbing the water that was on the side of his bed.

Zamari didn't know how long he's been here sleep but his throat was so dry right how he drunk the whole glass of water.

" I am Doctor Coii and your at Crest Care Hospital, do you remember what happened." He asked Zamari trying to see if he will have to take more scans of him.

"Only falling off the bed that's all" Mari told Doctor Coii looking around for Nayla. She was always by his side when they will sleep.

Before the Doctor could say anything else Mari interrupted him. "Where's Nayla" He asked trying to get up but his head started hurting.

"Hey easy, she's in the waiting room I will go get her and we will talk about what happened okay" Doctor Coii told Mari as he put his legs back in the bed for him.

"Okay" He replied looking at the tv on the wall that was playing Animal Discovery.

A baby chimpanzee will always be my favorite animal even though no face lady got her shit ate off doesn't mean that's going to happen to me,I mean I hope not.

"Mari"

He turned his head around so fast with a smile on his face hearing Nayla voice, but soon turned into a frown when he seen her red puffy eyes.

"What's wrong" He asked Nayla scooting over so she could get in the bed with him.

"I'm sorry" She mumbled putting her face in his neck as she rubbed his ear. " I didn't mean to push you that hard Mari." She sniffed trying to hold in her cries.

"I dont remember anything after I fell off the bed" He told Nayla removing her head from his neck as he rubbed her puffy eyes.

"Tell me what happened"

Nayla told Mari everything that happened the best she could without crying, she knew this was 100% percent her fault that Mari was in the hospital.

" I love you s-so much, I thought I lost you Mari" Nayla cried in Mari arms as he cradled her head.

"Y-You love me" He asked Nayla lifting up her head looking in her eyes. " Yes...soo much" Nayla responded leaning forward to kiss him.

Mari grabbed the back of Nayla neck with a firm grip as he tongue her down.

He knew he loved Nayla he was just so scared to say it back, because what if she didn't love him how he loved her.

" I love you so much more Nana" He told her putting his forehead on hers as he still gripped her neck.

Nayla and Zamari just looked in eachother eyes with soo much adoration,from anyone else eyes it would look like they been dating for some years .

□□ □□□□

"Here are some pills for your head." Nayla told Mari heading him the they gave him for his headache.

Mari was diagnosed with TBI (traumatic brain injury) So he has to take pills so the seizures wont just happened unexpectedly during the day. Nayla really hoped that she didn't ruin his life because of a mistake she made.

"Hey I'm okay" Zamari grabbed the pills out her hand and hugging her knowing she's still blaming herself for what happened.

Nayla wrapped her arms around his torso hugging him tightly happy that he's okay.

"Baby your phone is ringing" She told him moving back. Mari looked down at his phone weird because nobody doesn't call his phone and it was a private number.

"Hello"

"Let's meet we have to talk" Tay spoke through the phone.

i'm so happy that i got everything written out because my brain literally went blank and him having a seizure was definitely wasn't supposed to happened.

yes vote and comment.

twenty-five

"I haven't spoke to you in a while" Tay told Mari as they sat down in the mall.

Zamari is still surprised that Tay even called him,he thought he wouldn't hear from him again.

"Yeah the last 2 months has been crazy" Mari told him drinking his peach lemonade. " I want to explain to you what's been happening okay"

"Okay"

Tay had to make sure nobody was listening in on they conversation so he pulled his chair up closer.

Tayvon barley remember his parents,at the age of 9 his parents were killed. They was working for a guy who they know as "The Reaper".

His parents started to steal money from him trying to move to another country with they son, but soon enough The Reaper found out and ofc killed them. The Reaper took Tay under his wing every since then. Now Tay has been working off his parents debt

"Before they passed away they gave me this to chip they told me this was my way to freedom, but i'm not smart like you." Tay told Mari handing him the small chip trying to not look suspicious.

"What I do once I figure it out" He told Tay holding the chip in his hand really trying to see if this was a good idea or not. "Your little girlfriend is a Detective she can help" Tay spoke him with a smirk.

"How-" Mari couldn't finish his sentence because there was 2 big ass security guards asking him to get up from his seat.

"What for" Mari asked genuinely confused on what's going on.

"We got an anonymous tip that you are planning to bomb the mall." One of the guys spoke pulling him up out the seat.

□□□□□□□□ □□□□ □□□ □□□□ ? □□ □□ □□□□ 1963, □□.

"Keep it safe" Tay told Mari kissing his forehead before they pulled him away.Mari was pretty sure they had to be "The Reaper" guys so the only safe place right now was his mouth if they are going search him.

Mari pretended like he was coughing before putting the small chip in his mouth swallowing it. This chip will only come out off 2 ways hopefully it comes up the 1st way.

He felt a buzz in his pocket before carefully pulling out his phone seeing that they already had they hand on they gun.

-□□ □□□□.. Outside hurry up

Mari read over the message before hearting it.

"Oh god" He muttered before he turned around heading for the exit of mall, trying not bump into anyone.

"HEY STOP RIGHT NOW" The security guy yelled causing Mari to cover his left ear. Never in his life thought he would be running from a damn security guards with a chip in his body that felt that it was starting to come up.

"When I said hurry up I didn't mean ru-DRIVE" Mari stopped Nayla halfway through her sentence breathing heavy clutching his chest.

"What happened" Nayla asked Mari slowing down her speed seeing she was entering one of the neighborhoods who had the most kids that would be playing around.

" I will t-tell you later but right now...I think I gotta throw up"

this one is a little short ii might double update today though.

twenty-six

"Mari talk to me" Nayla spoke worriedly looking at Mari who looked like he could pass out any moment now.

"Y-Yeah just hurry up and park" He told her grabbing the handle slanging the door open running towards the door.

"YOUU FUCKING GORILLA SLANGING MY DOOR OPEN LIKE THAT" She yelled laughing at Mari who ran through the front door holding his mouth.

Nayla turned the car off dying laughing at the way he was running. She walked right through the door because he left the door open.

"YOU DIDNT EVEN TAKE OFF YOUR SHOES" She yelled again taking off her shoes by the walk-in table carrying her purse upstairs with her.

"Baby what's going on, are you sick" She asked rubbing his back as he continued to vomit. "No I have something you might want to see....that's if the shit come out" Nayla stop rubbing his back looking at him with disgusting look on her face.

"You have something that's literally in your body that I want to see" She asked looking at him confused now.

"Yeah" He responded out of breathe. Mari grabbed some tissue holding it to his mouth because he felt the the chip coming up.

"Mari why did you swallow that little ass thing" She mugged the back of his head.

"Tay gave this to me, this is for you Nana" He told her cleaning off the chip the best as he could handing it to her.

"Okay umm what he want me to do with this, he didn't tell you anything" She asked him inspecting the chip that look like you can possibly fit inside her computer that she has at home.

"Now my head hurts" He groaned flushing the toilet getting his toothbrush to brush his teeth.

"What did you eat yo shit stank" Nayla laughed walking out the bathroom, checking in on Dino.

"You literally always sleep there's no way you tired" Nayla spoke out loud post him on her story.

□□□□□□□□□□ • □□

"You okay now" She asked Mari taking off her shirt and pants putting them in the dirty clothes basket.

"Yeah I just want to cuddle now" Mari told her picked up Dino putting him in his dog bed downstairs.

"I have something to tell you" Nayla spoke getting under the covers resting her head on her hand while she watch Mari take off his clothes.

Lord knows she had to stop herself from grabbing his dick that was MOST DEFINITELY looking at her.

"Why you looking at me like that" He asked laughing a little getting in the bed turning towards her.

"You just so fine that's all" She chuckled looking in his eyes just staring at him for about a good 2 minutes.

"Fuck it" Mari muttered before grabbing her by her hair pressing his lips onto hers.

lmfaooa ii had something ta say but ii deadass forgot.

twenty-seven

Mari moved his hands from her hair grabbing Nayla neck shocking her at the new movement. Mari has been reading so he can catch up with Nayla,he wanted to pleasure her how she pleasure him.

"Mhmm baby where did you learn that" Nayla moaned with a small smile on her face with her arms wrapped around his neck as he positioned his-self between her legs.

"Books,they are really helpful you know" He told her trailing his hands down her stomach playing with her bellybutton.

"Yeah I see" She whispering grabbing the back of his neck kissing him deeply, moaning feeling his tongue touching hers.

Mari placed his hand on her pussy feeling how warm and wet she was. "ZaMari" Nayla moaned in his mouth feeling Mari rubbing her covered pussy.

Mari starting kissing on her jaw down to her kissing neck as he continued to rub over her pussy. "Should I stop" He asked looking at Nayla who had her bottom lip between her teeth with low eyes.

"Please dont" She whispered moaned loving the feeling of his kisses on her skin as he played with her pussy.

Mari continued to kiss on her neck adding his tongue which caused him to start suck on her neck pulling her underwear to side as he rubbed his fingers up and down her wet slit.

"Is this okay" He asked making sure he was doing it correctly, "Yes baby your doing so good" Nayla moaned sitting up on her elbows so she can watch him.

Mari unbuckled her bra throwing it somewhere in the room connecting his mouth to her light brown nipples as he play with the other one hearing Nayla moan out in pleasure.

"Mhmm just like that Mari" She moaned rubbing the back of his neck throwing her head back, " I g-gotta cum" She whispered feeling the tightness in her stomach.

Nayla never knew pleasure like this, it's just everything little thing he did she could just cum right there.

"Hold it Nana I want to taste it" He pouted kissing her lips repeatedly. He pulled Nayla to the end of the bed getting on his knees grabbing one of her legs putting it on his shoulders.

Mari kissed the inside of Nayla thighs getting closer to her pussy. "Baby stop playing please" She moaned trying not to release the knot in her stomach.

Mari pulled her underwear down to her ankles seeing all her substance cover her pussy. He put the part that covers her pussy in his mouth as he look in her eyes enjoying the flavor.

"Mhmm you taste so good." He moaned licking over his lips spreading her pussy lips seeing she was pink..like bubblegum pink.

He could see her pussy clenching around nothing which was making his dick hard just thinking about how her pussy would clench around his dick.

Mari connected his mouth with her clit,causing Nayla to throw her head back with her eyes closed and her mouth slightly opened."Fuckkk" she moaned lifting her head up as she watch him eat her pussy.

"You so pretty lala" Mari told her began to suck on the lower part of her pussy lifting one hand to grab her nipples pulling on them.

Nayla moaned again rubbing his head grinding her pussy on his face.

"Joder, Joder, Joder" Nayla moaned again pulling at his hair grinding her pussy on his face.(Fuck,Fuck,Fuck).

Nayla pulled his hair so tight that me moaned causing the vibration going straight to her pussy.

Her eyes begin to roll to the back of her head as she continued to grind her pussy on his face feeling his nose rub between her pussy lips rubbing against her clit.

As he continued, a creamy substance starts to leak out of her causing her leg to shake,Mari groaned against her as he sucks the cream from her pussy.

"O-Okay baby that's enough" Nayla moaned trying to push him back as he continues to eat her pussy adding 2 finger inside her rotating them in a slow pace.

"Voy a correrme de nuevo" She cried out falling on her back closing her legs as she released for the 2nd time. "Mari please" Nayla cried out pushing his head back.(I'm going to cum again)

"Damn" He spoke kissing her swollen pink pussy loving every second of it. "That squirting shit is such a turn on" He smiled her slapping her pussy a couple of times making her hips jerk

"Zamariiiiiii" She dragged out putting her hands on her face.

if anyone from my school see this...well ummm. yeah it wasn't me ii swea.

and ii used google for the translation sooo yeah.

twenty-eight

"Okay i'm going to tell you the surprise now" Nayla spoke washing the dishes after her dinner.

After they little moment they took a shower and fixed both of them some food because it was almost 7:00.

"Damn that was some good ass food but yes" He smiled helping her with the dishes. "I know this might sound a little weird but I sized your ear in your sleep to get you a custom hearing aid made" She told him turning towards him to see his reaction.

"A custom one" Mari whispered with a small smile on his face, really happy that she love him that much to get him a custom hearing aid for him.

Mari realized that the hearing aid had to be a lot of money." That's a lot of money though" He spoke drying his hands off.

"I know" She shrugged her shoulder not really caring about the price, if he needed a new one she was gon pay for it.

"Anyways when you gon get in the studio" She gave him a little smirk, knowing that he be writing in his notebook.

"I dont know really" He sighed as he dry the dishes off putting them up. " Tomorrow you gon get in the studio" She told him being serious, Mari was gon get in that studio.

Mari smiled loving how caring she was towards him, he will forever love her.

"I love you Nana"

"I love you more stink"

□□□ N□□□ □□□

"You ready" She spoke giving him a big smile turning off her car. " Stop smiling you gon make laugh and ion want to laugh" He told her trying to keep a straight face but end up laughing.

"Omg you so fine i'll suck yo dick rn" She faked cried rubbing over his dick through his pants. "Nayla" He spoke with a shocked expression not expecting to hear that from her.

"What I'm just saying" She laughed getting in her phone. " Get out now" He pointed towards the door with disappointment, surprised she said that.

"Let me take your picture stink" She told him getting out the car with her purse and a bottle of water.

□□.□□□□□□□□□

Liked by □□□□□□□□□□□ and 19,100 others □□.□□□□□□□□□ : 2nd to none. comments disabled

□

□

◻

"Nana can we talk" He asked her putting down his jar of peanut butter on the night stand. "Omg you cheated on me" She dramatically fell on the bed fake crying.

"Umm no but that's what I want to talk about,like are we together" He asked watching Nayla sit up with a now serious face. " I mean ye-yeah that's if you want" She stuttered getting nervous.

" I mean in my head we was married and all" He spoke making Nayla laugh playfully hitting him. " You ain't have to hit me" Mari spoke side eyeing her.

" Shut THE fuck up" She rolled her eyes. "Would you like to be my boyfriend Zamri" She asked laying her head on his thigh looking up at him.

" No"

goodmorning.

twenty-nine

"No" I respond just joking with Nayla. "What you mean no Mari" Nayla responded getting out the bed walking towards her closet.

"I mean I dont wanna be with you Nana" I told her rubbing my ear as I got out the bed" Well you shit out of luck" She responded walking out the closet with her own custom glock 19 in her hand looking dead serious.

"Nayla what are you doing" He asked surprised seeing her literally with a gun. " Oh nothing just being prepared" Nayla told him shrugging her shoulders walking towards him with a smile on her face with her gun still in her hand.

"For what" Mari gulped nervously as he backed up as she got closer causing him to fall on the bed. Nayla climbed on top of him sitting directly on his dick as she trailed her gun over his jaw.

"Baby watch it" He spoke nervously scared the gun might go off. " It's on safety baby Mami got this" She whispered the last part in his ear grinding on him.

Nayla pushed Mari all the way down on his back as she connected her mouth with the vein on the side of his neck as she trailed the gun down his stomach stoping at his V line.

Mari turned his head side ways giving her more access, grabbing her ass grinding her on his dick letting out little moans.

" You want this baby" Nayla asked grinning her hips with Mari pace biting her bottom lip trying to keep in her moans. " Yes I want it soo bad" He whined bucking his up a few times moaning as he released his nut in his shorts.

" Mhmm baby you wasn't supposed to do that yet." She moaned feeling his warm cum as she slowly grind on him. "I'm sorry it just felt so good"

" It's okay, take off all your clothes baby" Nayla commanded getting off his lap putting her gun next to his peanut butter.

She still have no clue as to why he's obsessed with peanut butter.

"Will it hurt when I loose my virginity" He asked sitting on the edge of the bed sliding his hands up and down his dick.

"No baby and stop doing that" Nayla took his hands putting them on her now naked waist trailing them up to her titties circling around her nipples. "Mhmm just like that"

Nayla trailed his left hand up to her mouth just giving him little kisses while her eyes was closed. She opened her eyes putting 2 finger in her mouth sucking them pretending it's his dick while giving him eye contact.

"Fuck" Mari moaned loving how she was taking his fingers. "Your leaking Mari" Nayla whispered taking his fingers out her mouth opening her legs rubbing them over her now wet pussy.

Nayla took her other hand bending down taking Mari pre-cum on her finger putting them in her mouth moaning at how good he taste, this shit was so damn good.

She took a big load putting them towards Mari. "Open,taste how good you is" She moaned still using Mari hand to rub her pussy.

Mari slowly opened his mouth sticking his tongue out as Nayla shoved her fingers in his mouth rotating them a little loving how much of a good boy he was.

"Your such a good boy Mari" She told him taking her finger out his mouth putting them in her mouth.

Nayla removed his hand from her pussy pushing him back on the bed as she climbed back on top of him.

She grabbed his head with both of her hands kissing him slowly moaning in his mouth as she felt Mari circle her second hole. "Can you open your mouth" Nayla asked tilting his head up by his chin letting her spit fall in his mouth.

Nayla reached behind her grabbing his dick sliding it up and down her wet folds teasing them both.

" Nana plea-Fuck please put it in" Mari practical cried wanting to be inside of her already."You ready" She asked pushing him in only a little moaning at the contact.

Maybe this wasn't the right position to be in because he's pretty big.

"Yes yes yes" He moaned putting his hands on her hips rubbing them in a soothing manner trying to be patient. As Nayla pushed him in Mari moaned feeling how tight and wet her pussy is.

Nayla was going to slow for Mari liking so he tightened his hands on her waist slamming her down on his dick causing them both to moan out loud.

ii will be skipping a lot because why not AND ion need only 1 person to be commenting throughout the whole book. ii get that yah are ghost readers but damn show a bitch you like the book.

thirty

I moaned out loudly putting my head in Mari neck biting him softly. " Baby Fu-Oh my god" I moaned as Mari moved my hips up and down at a steady pace.

Nayla could hear Mari letting out little groans every time she went down. Nayla sat up a little putting her hands around Mari neck adding a little pressure as she went up and down.

"Yes Nayla" Mari mumbled smacking her ass making Nayla moan throwing her head back. " Mierda Mari" Nayla whispered slowing down her pace. (Shit Mari)

"Nayla why you slowing down" Mari asked grabbing her waist again. "Baby I- wait" She whined standing on her tip toes.

Mari flipped them over so Nayla was up under him. "Open" He spoke tapping her things spreading them open.

Nayla opened her legs spreading her pussy lips giving Mari a beautiful view of her clenching pussy. " You gon put it in" He asked just seeing if she was going to do it.

Nayla reached down grabbing his dick teasing her hole pushing him in and out, she finally pushed him all the way in closing her legs grabbing the sheets as she scream out.

Mari pushed her legs open in a butterfly position holding her knees as he sliding in and out of her slowly. " Yes baby just like that" Nayla moaned biting her bottom lip leaning on her elbows to watch him.

"This pussy is so tight Nani" He groaned throwing his head back speeding up at his pace. "Mhmmm baby slow do-down" Nayla choked on her words putting her hands on his stomach feeling him hitting her g-spot.

"Mhm that's yo spot Nana" He whispered in her ear grabbing her neck keeping her legs open. " Yes baby right there" She moaned putting her arms around his neck as he picked her up slamming her on his dick.

The whole room was filled with both of they moans and skin clapping. Nayla pussy was leaking with her fluids making it super easy to slide into her.

Mari grabbed her thighs lifting her all the way up slamming her back down on his dick in a fast rhythmic pace. "I'm gonna cum baby' She cried out holding his neck for dear life.

"Hold it Nana" He whispered kissing her neck slowing down rolling his hips making sure Nayla could feel him. " I-I can't" She sniffed trying to control her tears from all the pleasure.

"Yes you can, I love you" Mari told her before slamming her back down on his dick causing Nayla to cry out stuttering I love you over and over again.

"Fuckkkkkk. Mar-" She cut herself off gasping loudly as she being to squirt. "Damn ain't know you could do that" He chucked pumping himself in her a few more times before he felt his stomach starting to tighten up.

"Mhmm baby where you want it" He asked heavily breathing trying to wait for her response. Nayla couldn't answer because she felt another orgasm coming.

Mari moved both hands around Nayla neck fucking her faster felling his his-self bout to come.

"Oh shit-fuck fuck Nayla baby" Mari moaned releasing at the same time as Nayla.

"Oh my god" Nayla whimpered with a small pout on her lips. " I know baby I-Im sorry" He repeatedly kissed her temple scared that he might have hurt her.

"It's okay bug I loved it"Nayla laughed speaking lowly because her voice was going out.

"I'm still sorry though" Mari spoke walking them towards the bathroom still connected.

"I'm going to pull out now okay" He warned her knowing that she was going to be sore.

"Wait just a few more minutes" She whispered putting her face in his neck getting sleepy. "Okay a few more minutes okay" He bounced her lightly walking back and forth to the bathroom to they room

" I will love to be your boyfriend Nayla"

well....

thirty-one

Nayla squirmed around in her sleep felling something wet on her pussy. "Mhmm fuckk" Nayla scratchy voice spoke as she released the knot in her stomach.

"Goodmorning" He whispered kissing her pussy feeling sorry about what happened last night.

"Morning baby" She wiped her eyes pulling him up kissing Mari tasting herself on his tongue.

"How many books did you actually read" She chuckled rubbing over his lips. "A lot but breakfast is ready fat girl" He whispered kissing her forehead.

"You know how to cook" She asked raising her eyebrows at him heading to us the bathroom. "Yes, I just dont cook" He spoke trailing behind her playing with her messy hair.

"So you been living with me for some months and never once told me you can cook...that's great" She gave him a sarcastic smile getting some feminine wipes to clean herself.

"I didn't think I needed to tell you honestly" He whispered in her neck roaming his handing over her body as she washed her hands.

Mari grabbed her by the back of her neck bending her over the counter pretending to give her back shots.

"Zamari unhand me" She laughed removing his hands from her neck. " I can't believe your mines it's crazy" He told her kissing her neck.

"Well believe it and get out i'm going to take a shower now" She turned around and hugged him before pushing him out.

"Omg I can't breathe" Mari dramatically clutched on his chest breathing heaving. "Mari get out damn im not going to take long" She laughed at how dramatic he was being.

"Fine"

☐

☐

☐

"Your going to starting cooking breakfast for now on because why is this good" Nayla told him eating her cheese grits. "Okay I would love to cook for you any day" He smiled at her.

Mari started playing with his food wanting to tell Nayla about the numbers. They haven't talked about the chip or the numbers and now he thinks it's time.

"I think it's time to talk about the whole point of why i'm here" He spoke clearly the rest of his food in the trash. "The numbers right" She asked making sure they was on the same page taking his plate from his hands sitting them in the sank.

"Yeah them fucking number" He muttered waking towards the living room thinking about them damn numbers. "What about the numbers" She asked putting her legs up under her as she sat on the couch.

Nayla and Mari both turned towards the back door hearing Dani growling at his chew toy outside.

"It's a long boring number" He told her looking over at the cartoon show that was playing as he rubbed his ear. "Presta atención" Nayla snapped her fingers at him gaining his attention(Pay attention)

"I can tell it you if you want" He shrugged his shoulders, " It wouldn't mean anything to me baby but how do you know it's one number and not a bunch of separate numbers" She asked trying to understand.

"Is there anything interesting to you about these numbers baby" Nayla asked Mari grabbing his hands, seeing he wasn't talking anymore probably thinking. "Maybe just a few of them"

"Okay why" She asked, "They either have a 3 or 8 before them,all the numbers are random but 5 of them have 8 before it and 7 of them have 3 before it" He told remembering the numbers clear as day.

"Nayla that's too many times to be random" Mari told her grubbing over her soft hands. "It's a code probably, was there anything else" She asked bringing his hands to her mouth to give him them a kiss.

"No nothing else"

"Soo it's the 3 and the 8 that are interesting" She asked herself almost putting the pieces together. "Just because they happened to many times to be random" He asked now confused.

"No it's because they aren't just numbers they are words" She told him looking into his brown eyes.

ion want this book ta end just yet but it's ending soon.

thirty-two

N ayla got up walking towards the walk-in table looking for a pen and a sheet of paper.

Where's the pen when you need it.

"Nana what are you doing" He asked confused as to why she's running all over the place. " I told you they are not just numbers they are words, right-left or left-right"

Mari was good with numbers and shit but this he had no fucking clue what was going on.

"Old school combination to a safe" She told him walking into the kitchen. "How you know this" He asked surprised that she was understanding this.

"My parents" She smiled walking back towards him with a pen and paper in her hand handing it to him.

"Just right down the numbers, only the ones with 3 and 8 infront of them" Nayla told him running up the stairs to get her MacBook pro off the charger.

Nayla ran back downstairs breathing heavily tired from all that damn running. " Okay-shit okay i'm going to put this chip into my computer and sees what pops up" She told him keeping him in the loop.

Nayla pulled up the carpet using her nail to lift up the floorboard reveling the chip along with passport and money.

Mari looked at her weirdly because why she has money and passport stashed in her floorboard hidden under a carpet.

Nayla seen his facial expressions and had to let him know.

"It's nothing bad I promise, I will explain later" She replied giving him a small smile grabbing the chip putting it in the computer.

Nayla turned on her computer before the MacBook went black for a second, then red letters just started rolling down the screen like a code or something.

The letters all of a sudden stop making just showing a red skin.

Nayla and Mari look at each other with a confused look.

"Well that wasn't at all creepy" Mari spoke with sarcastic tone getting up walking into the kitchen grabbing a strawberry cheesecake danish.

Nayla put down the computer on the coffee table following Mari. " I can't believe I really thought something was going to happen" She laughed biting his danish.

"Nayla" Mari calmly spoke looking at her with a irritated look on his face. "What and stop looking at me like you hate me" She rolled her eyes grabbing her a danish putting it on a plate putting it in the microwave.

"How you gon bite mines and then go fix you one" He asked with a mugged on his face. "Mari I'm sorry okay" Nayla laughed again taking the danish out the microwave sitting it down on the counter.

"You think it's funny"Mari asked with a raised eye seeing that her face was turning red from laughing so much. "No-No Mari it's not funny" Nayla responded trying to stop herself from laughing but her tears started clouding her vision which caused her to laugh out loud.

"Bye Nayla because ion find shit funny" He chucked shaking his head eating his half biting danish.

"Ma-" Nayla Macbook cut her off, "Here are your coordination" Read Out Loud from the computer.

Zamari and Nayla both ran into the living seeing the computer reading the same coordinations over and over again.

42.3314° N, 83.0458° W

"Nana write it down" Mari told her handing Nayla the paper and pen.

As soon as she was done the whole computer shut off.

thirty-three

August 2020

Today is August 26, which means it's Zamari birthday.

It's currently 2:30 in the morning and Nayla and her parents are in the living room decorating so when he wakes up he can see it.

Dino is sleeping ofc.

Her parents volunteered to help Nayla and later on today her parents will finally meet Mari a proper way this time.

"Okay you guys know his hearing is bad in one ear" Nayla told her parents so they know not to be loud when they going to tell him happy birthday.

"Poor baby do I need to buy him something because you know I will" Katherine asked worryingly. Michael chuckle shaking his head know his wife was being serious.

"No thanks Mama I got him a custom hearing aid one right here" Nayla smiled grabbing the hearing aid out of the box. His hearing aid came in 2 days ago but she wanted it to be his birthday surprise.

"Damn he got some big ass ears" Michael spoke picking up the hearing aid carefully.

"Papa" Nayla smacked his arm playfully grabbing the hearing aid from him.

"That wasn't very nice mi amor" Katherine spoke grabbing his ear. "Vale, vale, vale" Michael groaned in pain from the harsh grip. (Ow okay okay)

Katherine let go his ear giving him a harsh glare. Nayla laughed at her father who has a red face rubbing his ear.

"He's finally turning 19 what you got planned today" Katherine asked excitedly, they knew the age gap between Mari and Nayla.

They support her and they couldn't really do anything even if they didn't support her relationship because she's grown.

"We going out to eat he never been before" Nayla spoke smiling to herself thinking of him. "Okay let's go see the birthday boy" Katherine spoke with a smile on her face ready to go see Mari for the first time.

"Wait let's just see if he has any clothes on first" She spoke fast running up the stairs not wanting to hear what her parents have to say.

Nayla opened the door to they bedroom walking softly into the room seeing Dino curled up on Mari side.

"Aww if only he would sleep next to me like that" She rolled her eyes thinking of how much Dino betrayed her.

Dino head was on Mari torso as he slept on his side. Nayla pulled the bottom of the covers up seeing he had on some shorts.

She carefully turned back around heading out the door.

"Okay let's go" She spoke walking down the stairs seeing her parents damn near eating eachother face off.

"Mamá, papá, Dios mío, no está en mi casa, por favor" Nayla covered her eyes not wanting to see her parents kissing. " That was your mom, you know she li-" (Mom, Dad, my God, not in my house, please)

"Dad please stop it ewww" Nayla faked gagged walking past her parents to grab his gift. "I'm just saying-"

"Dad no more okay now let's go please"

"Una historia para otro día" Michael shrugged his shoulder. "No dad not a story for another day ion wanna hear it at all" She laughed heading upstairs with her parents trailing behind her.

Nayla pushed open seeing Dino is now laying on Mari stomach still sleeping. " Awww look at Dino" Katherine spoke holding her checks in adoration.

"Ain't no aww ma he dont even be on me like that"

"Stop whining he will come around later" Katherine spoke waving her off. "Ion think he will my love" Michael "tried" to whispered in Katherine's ear.

"Papá, lo escuché muy claramente" She turned around squinting at her dad. " Sorry" He whispered with a nervous smile. (Papa I so very clearly heard that)

Nayla moved Dino off Mari stomach holding him in her arms as he continues to sleep. "1.2.3 Cumpleaños feliz te deseamos a ti cumpleaños Mari cumpleaños feliz." Nayla and her parents started singing happy birthday to Mari loud enough so he could hear it.

Mari started waking up out of his sleep rubbing his eyes. Nayla put Dino on the floor because he was wide awake now.

"Happy birthday" Nayla sat on bed besides Mari as he continues to rub his eyes. " Huh" Mari spoke literally confused.

"It's your birthday and my parents are here" She whispered the last part in his ear.

Mari looked over to his left to see Nayla parents, well her mom smiling at him.

"Nayla this is so embarrassing" He spoke pulling the cover up on his body because he wasn't wearing a shirt. "It's not they just wanted to meet you and wish you a happy birthday"

"Happy birthday Zamari hopefully we can properly meet when your not half sleep" Katherine laughed looking at Mari who was laying his head on Nayla shoulder.

"Thank you and i'm sorry" He spoke picking his head up. " It's okay we kinda did wake you up at 3 in the morning.

"Happy birthday Kid." Michael spoke holding his side because his wife had pinched him for how mean he was looking towards Mari.

this was been supposed to go up at like 2.and any mistakes lmk. (let me know)

"Are you ready for date night" Nayla asked Mari walking out her parents house. They didn't sleep til 6 in the morning because Mari had others plans.

As soon as they woke up and got ready for today they went to Katherine and Michael house to have a small celebration for Mari.

Tay hasn't called or text him all day to tell him Happy Birthday but he wasn't going to think much about it. He's turning 19 today but he hopes Tay is doing well.

"I mean you can eat what's in my pants" He told her walking to the passenger side opening the door for her.

"Zamari just hush" She laughed "You will love the restaurant and thank you" She smiled kissing him on the lips getting in.

"How do you feel about letting others know we are together." Nayla asked Mari as he was steeping into the car. "I mean people are going to state they opinions but we know what we are."

"So I can post you" She's asked just to be clear. "Yes Nani you can post me" He laughed a little leaning over to kiss her forehead.

"I'm gonna go home so we can change okay"

□□□□□□□□□□□

•

Liked by □□□□□□□□□□□□ and 34,670 others □□□□□□□□□□□ : Feliz cumpleaños, cariño .comments off

□

□

□

"See look now we gon be late because you wanna play" Nayla breathe out picking up her purse making sure she had everything in there.

"Nani let's not put this on me okay, because you was the one that started grabbing my shit" He mugged her walking out the closet putting on his shoes.

"It was looking at me,what else I was supposed to do"

"Nani really y- never mind let's go" He laughed shaking his grabbing her hand.

□□□□□□□ □□□ ℝ□□□□□□□□□

"Baby can you take my pictures" Nayla asked Mari nicely handing him her phone.

"Damn" He mumbled watching Nayla do different poses. "Baby pay attention and take it" Nayla laughed seeing that Mari was just staring at her.

"My fault, come on" He told her licking his lips.

□□□□□□□□□□□

•

Liked by □□.□□□□□□□□□ and 23,670 others□□□□□□□□□□□ : not perfect but i'm the closest thing to it.comments off—Heading into the restaurant Mari was amazed there was big windows that had amazing views.

"Nani" Mari whispered looking around the place, he couldn't believe he was here in a fancy restaurant.

"Here are your seats" The host bowed towards them stoping at one of the tables that had the beautiful view." Thank you" Both Mari and Nayla replied loving how respectful they was.

"Nani are the seats spinning" Mari asked amazed seeing the building was slightly rotating in circles as he pulled out the chair for Nayla. "Yes they are, while we're eating we will be getting the whole view of Detroit"

"This shit is crazy man" She chuckled shaking his head sitting down instantly leaning on the window. "Now what if the window just brake and you fall out" Nayla spoke thinking out loud looking over the menu.

"Now why would you say that" Mari asked pushing his face off the glass scared that shit might really brake.

"Sorry I was just thinking out loud, but I'm going to order they Seafood and Chorizo Paella with Bell Peppers and Honey Garlic Salmon with Horseradish-Sour Cream Mashed Potatoes the share size bowl"

Mari looked up from his menu slowly.

"What" Nayla laughed watching Mari facial expression. "You getting all that food, Nani we probably wont even finish it all."

"It's okay we can take some home with us"She shrugged her shoulders stoping a waitress so they can order they food.

okay so this book is already finished.

should ii do a epilogue or not ?

thirty-five

"**Z**amari hold on to me okay" Nayla tried to hold Mari on her shoulders as she unlocked the door.

Let's just say Mari had too much wine and is now drunk asf.

Nayla finally unlocked the door dragging Mari inside the house trying to keep him up.

"Just stay right here okay I'm going to go get water" Nayla told him putting on the couch.

Nayla put her purse down on the kitchen counter walking toward the refrigerator to grab a bottle of water.

Nayla heard a thud sound making her turn around fast.

"Mari are you okay" She called out not getting a answer from him.

Nayla figured he must have dropped something on the floor so she grabbed her purse going upstairs to change her clothes.

She was going to get up out her dress first before she could handle him up.

In the process of putting on her bonnet she heard glass brake which caused her to pause her movement.

Nayla reached on the top shelf grabbing her gun out of the box just to be safe.

Dino was at her parents house right now.

She walked down stair slowly with her gun in her hand hearing grunting,Once she reached the bottom stairs she can see lights on in the living room.

Maybe Mari had turned on the lamp she thought.

"No" She heard Mari speak which made Nayla walk into the living room seeing Matt having Mari in a choke hold with a gun aimed to his head.

"Matt what the hell are youu doing"

"It wasn't supposed to go down like this but I need the code" Matt responded pushing Mari down on his knees.

Mari had no clue what's going on he's still drunk as hell.

"Matt what are you doing" She asked still having no clue what Matt is doing in her house.

"The code Nayla" He spoke shooting Mari in the arm. "MATT STOP" Nayla screamed pointing her gun at Matt.

Matt had a silencer on his gun so nobody has a clue what's going on besides them,Nayla couldn't believe this was actually happening right now.

"Matt isn't my name Nayla" He chucked shaking his head. "I been trying to get these damn NUMBERS CODES FOR YEARS NOW" He yelled shooting passed Mari head.

"Please just stop okay" She plead seeing Mari holding his arm loosing a lot of blood.

"He been supposed to die the minute he picked up the fucking paper" Matt spoke shooting Mari again in his leg making Nayla raise her gun.

"Shoot and I will kill him" Matt spoke pointing the gun at Mari head as he sat down in the armchair.

Mari wasn't drunk at all now which meant he felt everything, he was just having a good time to him now being shot.

"My name is Maurizio Bianchi bellissima" He smirk fixing his pants leg as he manspread. "See before my babbo passed he passed down his business down to me and now i'm over the business"

"Before he passed he gave me a piece of paper telling me to decrypt the code, So I moved down to Detroit because the Tijuana Cartel had someone for that" He spoke shaking his head.

"That was 6 years ago, So I joined the Detective route as a cover up."

"His pathetic friend parents was supposed to help but you know they got greedy and start stealing from me"

"Enough of the sad story okay just please leave he needs a hospital" Nayla tried to hold in her tears seeing Mari eyes slowly rolling to be back of his head.

"No you are going to listen to the whole story Nayla" He laughed like this shit was funny.

"Mari keep your eyes open okay" She spoke carefully walking towards Mari. "Step back before I shoot you next" Maurizio spoke aiming the gun at Nayla now.

Nayla backed away slowly keeping her eyes on Mari.

"Back to the story now" He spoke sitting his gun on his lap. "Once I found out they was stealing I of course killed them and took in they little bastard" He licked over his lips a little.

"A few years after his parents die I found the Triad Mafia and the results was very promising. We was making process but they had to fuck it up by dropping the FUCKING PAPER AND THIS PIECE OF SHIT JUST HAD TO PICK IT UP"Maurizio yelled kicking Mari because him to groan in pain.

"That's how we get here Na-"

A knock on the door stop Maurizio midway through his sentence which caused both of them to look towards the door.

As soon as Nayla started walking towards the door Maurizio let off a shot towards Nayla barely missing her head,Nayla shot back grazing his arm.

Hearing the shoot on the other end of the door Michael kicked the door down seeing his daughter ducking behind the couch and Mari on the ground unconscious.

Maurizio ran towards the bck door ducking shots as Nayka started emptying the clips hitting him twice in the shoulders.

"Mama,Papa go call 911" Nayla cried getting from up behind the couch walking towards Mari.

While Katherine called 911 Michael started doing CPR on Mari seeing he wasn't breathing and he didn't have a pulse.

"Come on kid" Michael spoke giving Mari 30 chest compressions.

Katherine was still on the phone with 911 updating them on what's going on.

Katherine sat on the ground behind Nayla hugging her seeing that her face was turning red.

"Va a estar bien, cariño" Katherine slightly rocking them back and forth trying to calm both of them down. (He's going to be okay baby)

rip Zamari.

thirty-six

"Today marks 47 days since you been in a coma Mari" Nayla spoke holding onto his hand seeing his chest move up and down.

Nayla moved in with her parents after weeks of Mari being in a coma.

Nayla hasn't been to work probably wont even return with all the news she found out about "Matt". She couldn't believe he was The Reaper.

"How are you doing Ms.Baptise" The nurse asked checking Mari vitals. Everyday the nurse would see Nayla cry over Mari bed everyday and just talk to him.

"I'm okay" She replied wiping her eyes occasionally rubbing over Mari hand.

"Everything is perfect he should be waking up soon okay" The nurse told her giving Nayla a small smile before leaving the room.

"Estoy deseando volver a ver tus hermosos ojos" (I can't wait to see your beautiful eyes again)

□□ □□□ □□□□□□□ R□□□□□□□□

"Kiddo it's almost 10 and you still haven't ate are you okay" Michael asked standing on the outside of the guest bedroom that Nayla turned into Mari and hers.

"Yeah i'm okay but I might have something" She spoke turning her computer around so he can see.

After the incident with Maurizio she went to follow the coordinates and they lead her to Treasury Bank Financial.

As she kept following the coordinates she found a specific lockbox #5681, she put in the code that was decrypted and found 30M dollars, another chip and another piece of paper.

Nayla stored the money in a storage unit but kept the paper and the chip.

Michael walked into the room sitting on the bed grabbing his glasses off top of his head putting them on.

"Nayla what is this" Michael seeing a lot of names and building.What was odd about this was that mostly of the building names and the people names wasn't in English.

"That is all different types of accounts and operations" She told him biting on her nails nervously.

"N-" Michael got cut off by Katherine busting into the room with heavy foot steps following behind her.

"Mama what's wrong" Nayla asked grabbing her glock off the nightstand. "4-6 guys just broke into the house" Katherine spoke breathing heavily.

"Hey breathe okay" Michael spoke walking towards Katherine who was staring to have a panic attack. "Look at me you have to breathe" He spoke trying to calm down his wife.

"Mama,Papa stay here while I go out there" She told her parents putting her hair in a bun. "Nayla no i'm going with you" Michael spoke still holding onto his wife.

"No mama need you, I will be back safely" She told her parents carefully opening up the door.

As Nayla walked out the room she see 2 people down the hall walking towards her parents room. She raised her gun letting off 2 shots hitting them both in the head.

Nayla walked towards the dead bodies heading downstairs. "Dov'è questa stronza?" She heard a voice spoke making her turn her head towards the living room.

"Over here" Nayla spoke making the guy turn his head towards her. Nayla waved at him before shooting him between his eyes.

Nayla turned her head around seeing a big ass guy walking out the kitchen with sandwich in his hand.

"Fat ass put the sandwich down" She spoke pointing the gun at him. Before he could even pull his gun out Nayla shot him in his leg,causing him to fall on the ground holding his leg.

"You bitch im going to kill you" He spoke with a heavy Italian accent reaching for his gun again.

"I wouldn't do that if I was you" She spoke kicking his gun out of his reach.

"What do you want" She asked him now standing over him. 'Suck my dick" He laughed holding his leg.

"What did you say to me" She asked with a raised eyebrow. "I SAID SUCK MY FUCKING DICK"

"Suck your own dick" She told him shooting him in his head.

2 more chapters other this den a epilogue.

thirty-seven

"Mama, Papa you guys have everything" Nayla asked her parents walking through the hotel.

They called the the police and left the scene for them to handle. This was currently living in the Fort Pontchartrain hotel.

Nayla just went back to her house to grab the rest of Dino and Mari things, including the things in the floorboard.

"Yes we are ready" Katherine spoke holding Dino up while Michael was carrying the bags to the car.

"Papa we have to go get Mari from the hospital he's not staying in there" She told her parents walking into the other bedroom.

Nayla had got a hold to a shot of Zolpidem, this was going to hopefully wake Mari up from his coma.

Nayla walked towards the door seeing both of her parents in the car holding hands as they pray.

□□ □□□□ □□ □□□□

"He's at the Crest hospital" She told her dad who was now placing kisses on her mother knuckles.

☐

☐

☐

"Kiddo I need you and your mother to stay in the car okay" Michael told Nayla looking back at her.

They was now parked by the backdoor of the hospital. Nayla couldn't carry Mari and Michael knew that so he was going to go get Mari.

"Papa"

"No papa nothing i'm going and that's final" He told her unbuckling his seatbelt getting out the car.

Nayla rolled down the window to give her dad the Zolpidem. "If he's not already woke give him this and he should wake right up"

"Okay" He spoke sticking his head through the window to give Nayla a kiss on her forehead.

"Be careful"

"I will kiddo I promise"

Katherine and Nayla sat in the car watching Michael walk through the exit door. All they they could do is pray that they make it out okay and nobody gets hurt.

It's been 15 minutes now and Nayla started to get worried,she kept looking at her watching counting as the minutes went by.

"Get out the car" Nayla heard a voice spoke as he pointed the gun at her mother window.

Katherine slowly got out the car with her hands up not wanting the guy to shoot her. Nayla knew he was going to kill her mother if she didn't kill him first.

As he turned his back towards the car walked behind Katherine Nayla rolled down the window and let off 3 shots.

"Mama get in" Nayla spoke nervously knowing people heard the shots and police will probably be on they way soon.

Nayla got out the car and grabbed the piece of paper out her pocket that she wrote just for Maurizio.

□□ □□□□□□□□ □□□□□*h*□

Here is twenty nine million,nine hundred and fifty thousand dollars. We will pay back the remaining 50 thousand,with interest. If you must know just in case your still angry, I know every account of every operation you have in Italy and the money routes back into Italy. You won't come after us we won't come after you. Come after us and your world ends. You have my word on that.

Michael walked out the door with Mari over his shoulders trying to keep his heavy ass up . "What happened here"

"Long story short they are still following us but after this im sure they will stop" She spoke walking towards the trunk."Mama pop it"

Nayla grabbed the bag of cash out the trunk sitting it on the dead guys chest right alone with the note.

Nayla got back inside the truck so her father can put Mari heads in her lap. "Hey" Mari whispered grabbing Nayla face.

"Hey" She replied trying to control her tears. With all the shit she been through she just couldn't do nothing but cry tears of joy.All this shit was finally over and they get they life on track.

"Where to Kiddo" Michael asked looking in the review mirror at Nayla.

"Salt Lake City"

ii really was gon kill Katherine ass. but ii changed my mind.

thirty-eight

S alt Lake City| Months later

"Can she hurry up and come out god" Nayla groaned grubbing her big baby bump.Her due date was June 28, it's now July 3 and she's s still not her.

"Maybe she will come out tomorrow, you know it's the 4th." Mari smirked eating a reese cup.

Nayla birthday is December 6 so she wanted to be pregnant before she turnt 27 because she feels like she's getting old, even though Mari doesn't think so.

"Stop all that smirking" She mugged him,"Tell your mama you will arrive tomorrow" Mari spoke to Nayla stomach getting a few kicks.

"Aww hell noo" Nayla laughed shaking her head.she was not planing on having a baby on the 4th.

Mari just started laughing like it was funny, this 4th of July was going to be so problematic.

"Let me go call my parents before I have to kill you."

"I'm sorry Nini,I love you"

"Yeah whatever Zamari I love you more."—

"Did you enjoy dinner" Nayla asked Mari as he lazily rubbing her stomach while they laid in bed.

When Mari found out Nayla was pregnant he was so excited but again scared because he didn't want his children to grow up getting bullied the same way he did.

Nayla told him even though they child did end up having SSHL they would still be loved the same and ain't nobody fucking with they child.

"Yeah, got my ass sleepy" He chuckled turning to lay on his side. "I can't wait to see who she look like"

"Probably your ass" Nayla rolled her eyes getting on her phone. "Why you had to roll your eyes though"

"Because I just know it" Nayla laughed shaking her head.

"Have you talked to Tay" She asked looking over at him. "Yeah he's doing good now that he isn't under Maurizio ass"

□□□□□□□□□□□

Liked by □□.□□□□□□□□□□ and 43,671 others□□□□□□□□□□□ : . Comments off

—July 4th| Baptise New Residents

"How is my grand-baby doing" Katherine asked with a smile on her face.

When she found out that she was having a grandchild she was too excited but with Michael it took some time to process that his only child is having a baby.

"She's doing fine,I keep catch theses annoying cramps though." She responded looking around for Mari.

Nayla been timing her cramps so she know if she needs to go to the hospital or not.

"If your looking for Mari,he's with your father having that guy talk they always do"She told Nayla linking they arms walking towards the food.

"Look at this food" Nayla smiled reaching for a meatball,Nayla paused hunching over feeling a sharp pain under her stomach. "You okay" Katherine asked tubbing her back.

"Yeah j-" Nayla couldn't finish her sentence because she felt water running down her legs. "My grand-baby is coming" Katherine spoke looking into Nayla eyes.

The rest of her family members went running around the house looking for Mari and Michael while others was prepared to have the baby at home.

"I'm not having the baby here so tell Abuelita to stop grabbing towels" Nayla laughed holding the bottom of her stomach scared to move.

"I told you she was coming on the 4th" Mari laughed walking towards Katherine sticking his hand out. "I'm literally going into labor and you guys are really doing this"

"Vale, vale, vamos" Michael spoke walking out the house with the extra baby bag they kept here and her car seat. (Okay okay let's go)

□

□

□

□□□□□□□□□□□

Liked by □□.□□□□□□□□□ and 56,461 others□□□□□□□□□□□ : 7/4/21.Com
ments off

—

□□.□□□□□□□□□

..

thirty-nine

S alt Lake City| Years Later

"Amina,Brynlee,Cali and Nayla can you girls hurry up" Mari asked nicely waiting on the girls to get ready. Today they are going to take the girls to Zoo, they been asking for longest.

After they had Amina they waited 1 years to have another child, they goal was to have a boy but you know they end up with another girl,Brynlee.

They tried again 2 years later and had Cali,they was excited to have 3 girls but they really wanted a little boy.

At some point Nayla wanted to giving up but Mari persuaded her to give it another try.

Before Cali turned 2 they tried again and now they have 4 month old baby boy name Daione.

"We are coming I had to feed Daione again and den change his diaper" Nayla spoke walking down the stairs holding Daione while the girls followed behind her holding hands carefully walking down the stairs.

"He's always eating" Mari spoke walking towards Nayla with Dino follow-ing behind him.

After all theses years Dino will still always be under Mari, but occasionally he will be in the kids room just watching them as they play or read a book.

"Mamá, ¿me puedes tom-mar un poco de mant-tequilla de maní, p-por favor?" Amia asked speaking her broken Spanish that Nayla is currently teaching all the kids. (Mama may I have some peanut butter please)

Fun Fact: Somehow Mari gots every child addicted to peanut butter.

"No baby but you can have peanut butter crackers" Nayla told Amina looking into her brown eyes that look so much like Mari.

"Can you hold him for a second please" Nayla asked Mari handing Daione towards him.

Nayla walked toward the kitchen of they new home, after they had Brynlee they moved into a 5 bedroom and a 4 bathroom house.

1 master bathroom, 2 full bathroom and 1 half bathroom downstairs.

They have this big office space but they dont use it so they turned it into the kids playroom.

"Here's your crackers and grab a bottle of water out the refrigerator okay and be careful"

"You want anything Bryn"

"y-es please" Bryn whispered with her stuffed animal towards her mouth blocking some of her words. Bryn wasn't shy but it's just she doesn't talk much and that was okay.

Nayla knew what she wanted so she walked towards the refrigerator to grab the pineapples. She cut up 3 whole pineapples into slices putting them into in her custom container with her name on it.

Nayla grabbed her a bottle of Cran•Grape knowing that was her favorite juice.

"□□□□□ □□□ □□□□ □□□□□□□□□ □□□□ □□□□ " Nayla signed to Cali.

Cali was born with unilateral hearing loss, it wasn't shocked that Cali was born deaf in one ear because Nayla and Mari knew this could happen to either one of they kids.

Cali can talk a little but she prefer to sign instead.

Zamari teaches Amina,Brynlee and Cali ASL or they just watch a few videos on yt together.

Everyday is getting better and better but it's difficult to keep a hearing aid in a 2 year old ear.

"□□□□□□□□□" Cali poorly signed but Nayla knew what she trying to sign.

Nayla pulled out the Italian bread out of the bread holding cutting a small portion of it slicing it in half like a sub sandwich,Next she grabbed all the things she knew Cali would love on her sandwich.

Cali might be small but she could eat, just like her parents.

Nayla grabbed Chipotle mayonnaise,Dijon mustard.Lettuce,Tomatoes,Pickles,Purple Onions and Pepper Jack cheese.

She pulled out Cali costume lunch box putting her sandwich inside with a bag of Dill Pickle Lays.

"□□□□□ □□□□□ □□□□□□" Cali asked looking up towards her mother still not letting go of Bryn hand.

Nayla grabbed a bottle of apple juice out the refrigerator putting that in her lunchbox also handing it to her.

"Okay Mari we are finally ready" Nayla spoke walking towards the living from seeing Mari taking pictures of Daione chubby self.

"Did you wake him up" She asked Mari seeing Daione is wide awake now in his car seat. "No of course not"

Nayla felt a tap on her leg and she look down seeing Cali sign to her, "□□ □□ □ □□□□" Cali signed laughing a little hiding behind Nayla legs seeing her dad shocked expressing.

"Really Cali I thought we was homies" Mari spoke slowly walking towards Nayla to tickle Cali.

"Mama are we going to go see uncle Tay and auntie Maddie" Amina asked walking over towards her baby brother.

Detective Maddie and Tayvon are together now, dont know how that happened but overall Mari and Nayla are happy for them.

"Yes my love we will meet them there"

"Cousins will b-be there a-also" Bryn whispered with her stuff animal still to her mouth.

"Mari stop tickling my baby" Nayla spoke picking up Cali kissing her now red face. "Yes baby they will be there also"—

www.ingramcontent.com/pod-product-compliance
Lightning Source LLC
Chambersburg PA
CBHW070402200726

48294CB00003B/1051